THE
Greatest
JOKE BOOK
EVER
T0115963

MEL GREENE

HARPER

NEW YORK • LONDON • TORONTO • SYDNEY

AVON BOOKS, INC.
1350 Avenue of the Americas
New York, New York 10019

Cover illustration by Chris Erkmann
Interior design by Kellan Peck
Published by arrangement with the author Bill Adler Books, Inc.
ISBN: 0-380-79849-2
www.avonbooks.com

Library of Congress Cataloging in Publication Data:

Greene, Mel.
The greatest joke book ever / Mel Greene.
p. cm.
1. American wit and humor. I. Title.
PN6162.G74 1999 99-36268
818'.5402—dc21 CIP

First Avon Books Trade Paperback Printing: November 1999

Printed in the U.S.A.

40 39 38 37 36

Contents

THE Greatest JOKE BOOK EVER

Airplanes

One day at a busy airport, the passengers on a commercial airliner are seated, waiting for the cockpit crew to show up so they can get under way.

The pilot and copilot finally appear in the rear of the plane and begin walking up to the cockpit through the center aisle. Both appear to be blind. The pilot is using a white cane, bumping into passengers right and left as he stumbles up the aisle, and the copilot is using a guide dog. Both have their eyes covered with huge sunglasses.

At first the passengers do not react, thinking that it must be some sort of practical joke. However, after a few minutes the engines start revving and the airplane starts moving down the runway.

The passengers look at one another with some uneasiness, whispering among themselves and looking desperately to the flight attendants for reassurance.

Then the airplane starts accelerating rapidly, and people begin panicking. Some passengers are praying, and, as the plane gets closer and closer to the end of the runway, the voices are becoming more and more hysterical.

Finally, when the airplane has less than twenty feet of runway left, there is a sudden change in the pitch of the shouts as everyone screams at once, and at the very last moment the airplane lifts off and is airborne.

Up in the cockpit, the copilot breathes a sigh of relief and turns to the pilot: "You know, one of these days the passengers aren't going to scream, and we're going to get killed!"

An airplane pilot died at the controls and promptly went to hell.

The devil took him to the "newly arrived" area, where there were three doors, marked 1, 2, and 3, in turn. The devil told the pilot that he was going to get to choose his own hell, but the devil had to take care of something first, and then he disappeared.

The curious pilot looked behind door number 1. He saw a pilot going through preflight checks for all eternity.

He looked behind door number 2 and saw a pilot who forever found himself trying to resolve the same emergency situations that had sent him to hell in the first place.

He looked behind the last door and saw a pilot being waited on hand and foot by scantily clad flight attendants.

The devil returned just as the pilot returned to his waiting position. The devil offered the pilot a choice of door number 1 or number 2.

The pilot said, "I wanted door number three!"

"Sorry," replied the devil. "That's flight attendant's hell."

While cruising at thirty thousand feet, the airplane shuddered and Mr. Benson looked out the window. "Good lord!" he screamed. "One of the engines just blew up!"

Other passengers left their seats and came running over; suddenly the aircraft was rocked by a second blast as yet another engine exploded on the other side.

The passengers were in a panic now, and even the flight attendants couldn't maintain order. Just then, standing tall and smiling confidently, the pilot strode from the cockpit and assured everyone that there was nothing to worry about.

His words and his demeanor seemed to make most of the passengers feel better, and they sat down as the pilot calmly walked to the door of the aircraft. There, he grabbed several packages from under the seats and began handing them to the flight attendants.

Each crew member attached the package to his or her back.

"Say," spoke up an alert passenger, "aren't those parachutes?"

The pilot said they were.

The passenger went on, "But I thought you said there was nothing to worry about?"

"There isn't," replied the pilot as a third engine exploded. "We're going to get help."

Seven Indicators That You Have Chosen the Wrong Airline:

1. Ground crew seen using pennies to check tire wear.
2. Upon closer inspection trendy desert-pastel paint job turns out to be primer yellow and Bondo pink.
3. Man with oily rag hanging from the back pocket of his dirty overalls turns out to be the pilot.
4. Voice on P.A. system warns you to keep your hands and arms inside the aircraft while it is in motion.
5. Just before takeoff, the flight attendant offers coffee, tea, or Valium.
6. Air sickness bags are printed with the Lord's Prayer.
7. Pilot asks if anyone on board has jumper cables with them.

Bars and Booze

The local bar was so sure that its bartender was the strongest man around that they offered a standing bet for $1,000.

The bartender would squeeze a lemon until all the juice ran into a glass, then hand the lemon to a patron. Anyone who could squeeze out one more drop of juice would win the money.

Many people had tried over time (weight lifters, longshoremen, etc.), but nobody could do it.

One day this scrawny little man came into the bar, wearing thick glasses and a polyester suit, and said, in a tiny squeaky voice, "I'd like to try the bet."

After the laughter had died down, the bartender said okay, grabbed a lemon, and squeezed away. Then he handed the wrinkled remains of the rind to the little man.

But the crowd's laughter turned to total silence as the

man clenched his fist around the lemon and six drops fell into the glass.

As the crowd cheered, the bartender paid the $1,000, and asked the little man, "What do you do for a living? Are you a lumberjack, a weight lifter, what?"

The man replied, "I'm an IRS agent."

The bartender was dumbfounded when a gorilla came in and asked for a martini, but he couldn't think of any reason not to serve the beast. And he was even more amazed to find the gorilla coolly holding out a ten-dollar bill when he returned with the drink.

As he walked up to the cash register, he decided to try something. He rang up the sale, headed back to the animal, and handed it a dollar in change. The gorilla didn't say anything—he just sat there sipping his martini.

Finally the bartender couldn't take it anymore. "You know," he offered, "we don't get too many *gorillas* in here."

And the gorilla replied, "At nine bucks a drink, I'm not surprised."

A ninth-grade chemistry teacher wanted to demonstrate the evils of liquor to his young students. He produced a glass of water, a glass of whiskey, and two worms.

"Now class, observe closely," he said as he dropped one of the worms into the glass of water. The worm wriggled about in the water, perfectly happy.

The teacher dropped the second worm into the glass of whiskey. The worm swam around for a moment, then seized up and curled, quickly sinking to the bottom of the glass, dead as a doornail.

"Now, what can be learned from this experiment?" the teacher asked his students.

After a pause, young Tom stood up and said, "Well, if you drink whiskey, you'll never get worms."

A man was feeling very depressed. He walked into a bar and ordered a triple scotch whiskey. As the bartender poured him the drink he remarked, "That's quite a heavy drink. Is something wrong?"

After quickly downing his drink, the man replied, "I got home today and found my wife in bed with my best friend."

"Wow," exclaimed the bartender as he poured the man a second triple scotch, "No wonder you needed a stiff drink. This one's on the house." As the man finished the second scotch, the bartender asked him, "So what did you do?"

"I walked over to my wife," the man replied, "looked her straight in the eye, and told her that we were through. I told her to pack her stuff and to get the hell out."

"That makes sense," said the bartender, "but what about your best friend?"

"I walked over to him, looked him right in the eye, and said, 'Bad dog!' "

The FDA is considering printing additional warnings such as these on beer and alcohol bottles:

WARNING: Consumption of alcohol may make you think you are whispering when you are not.

WARNING: Consumption of alcohol is a major factor in dancing like a jerk.

WARNING: Consumption of alcohol may cause you to tell the same boring story over and over again until your friends want to *smash your head in.*

WARNING: Consumption of alcohol may cause you to thay shings like thish.

WARNING: Consumption of alcohol may lead you to believe that ex-lovers are really dying for you to telephone them at four in the morning.

WARNING: Consumption of alcohol may leave you wondering what happened to your pants.

WARNING: Consumption of alcohol may cause you to roll over in the morning and see something really scary (whose species and/or name and/or gender you can't remember).

WARNING: Consumption of alcohol is the leading cause of inexplicable rug burns on the forehead.

WARNING: Consumption of alcohol may create the illusion that you are tougher, better looking, and smarter than some really, really big guy named Chuck.

WARNING: Consumption of alcohol may lead you to believe you are invisible.

WARNING: Consumption of alcohol may lead you to think people are laughing *with* you.

WARNING: Consumption of alcohol may cause an influx

in the time-space continuum, whereby small (and sometimes large) gaps of time may seem literally to disappear.

WARNING: Consumption of alcohol may actually *cause* pregnancy.

A man walks into a bar and orders a beer. After a few minutes he says to the bartender, "Hey if I show you the most amazing thing you've ever seen, will you give me another beer on the house?"

"We'll see," says the bartender. "I've had a lot of nuts come in here, and I've seen some pretty amazing things in my day."

So the man pulls out a hamster and a tiny piano from his briefcase and puts them on the bar. Then the hamster begins to play Chopin.

"Not bad," says the bartender, "but I'll need to see more."

"Okay, hold on," says the man as he pulls out a frog from his briefcase. Suddenly, the frog starts singing "My Way."

A patron nearby jumps up from his table and says, "That's amazing! I'll give you a thousand dollars right now for that frog."

"Sold!" says the man, who exchanges the frog for the cash.

The bartender then says to the man, "You know, it's none of my business, but I think you just gave away a real fortune in that frog."

"Not really," says the man, "the hamster is also a ventriloquist."

An angry wife was complaining about her husband spending all his time at the pub, so one night he took her along.

"What'll ya have?" he asked.

"Oh, I don't know. The same as you, I suppose," she replied.

So the husband ordered a couple of Jack Daniel's and threw his down in one go.

His wife watched him, then took a sip from her glass and immediately spit it out. "Yuck, it's nasty poison!" she spluttered. "I don't know how you can drink this stuff!"

"Well, there you go," cried the husband. "And you think I'm out enjoying myself every night!"

A man walked into a bar and ordered a glass of white wine. He took a sip of the wine, then tossed the remainder into the bartender's face.

Before the bartender could recover from the surprise, the man began weeping. "I'm really sorry. I keep doing that to bartenders. I can't tell you how embarrassing it is to have a compulsion like this."

Far from being angry, the bartender was sympathetic. Before long, he was suggesting that the man see a psychoanalyst about his problem. "I happen to have the name of a psychoanalyst," the bartender said. "My brother and my wife have both been treated by him, and they say he's as good as they come."

The man wrote down the name of the doctor, thanked the bartender, and left.

The bartender smiled, knowing he'd done a good deed for a fellow human being.

Six months later, the man was back. "Did you do what I suggested?" the bartender asked, serving the glass of white wine.

"I certainly did," the man said. "I've been seeing the psychoanalyst twice a week." He took a sip of the wine. Then he threw the remainder into the bartender's face.

The flustered bartender wiped his face with a towel. "The doctor doesn't seem to be doing you any good," he spluttered.

"On the contrary," the man said, "he's done me a world of good."

"But you just threw the wine in my face again!" the bartender exclaimed.

"Yes," the man said. "But it doesn't embarrass me anymore!"

A man went into a bar, already very, very drunk, hardly able to stand up, and slurring his words as he muttered to himself. At the bar, he called out, "Hey, bartender! Gimme a martini!"

"No, no," said the bartender. "You've had too much already."

The drunk spied a dartboard behind the bar.

"Tell you what," he said. "If I can throw three bull's-eyes with that dart set, would you gimme a drink?"

"Sure," said the bartender, certain the guy would

leave after the little game. He handed the drunk three darts and warned, "Look out, everybody!"

Zot, zot, zot. The drunk threw three quick bull's-eyes.

The bartender had never seen anything like that before, but he had to make good on the wager, so he made a martini and set it before the drunk. He then put a napkin next to the drink and set a turtle on it.

"What's this?" asked the drunk.

"That's a prize we give out for such fine dart throwing," said the bartender.

The drunk drank his martini in one gulp, picked up the turtle, put it in his coat pocket, and left.

The next night, the same drunk went into the same bar, again totally inebriated.

"Bartender," he said. "Gimme a martini!"

"No, no," says the bartender. "You're too drunk again. Go home."

Again the drunk noticed the darts.

"If I can throw three bull's-eyes, would you gimme the martini?" he asked.

The bartender thought, This guy can't be that lucky again. I'll get rid of him. "Sure, sure," he said, handing over the darts.

Bip, bip, bip. Three bull's-eyes again.

"Holy cow," said the bartender, and he gave the drunk guy a martini. Again, he set a turtle next to the drink.

"What's this?" asked the drunk.

"That's a prize for being such a good shot."

"Oh," said the drunk, and he quaffed his martini, put the turtle in his coat pocket, and left.

The very next night the same drunk came into the same bar.

"Gimme a martini!" he demanded.

"No, no," said the bartender. "You've been overserved already. Get on home."

Spying the dartboard once more, the drunk guy said, "Would tossing three bull's-eyes prove that I'm not overserved?"

The bartender couldn't believe that anybody this drunk could possibly hit the dartboard, let alone get three bull's-eyes, let alone do so three nights in a row.

"Okay," the bartender agreed, once again forking over the three darts.

The drunk deftly grabbed all three darts and tossed them simultaneously.

Thwock! All three darts landed solidly in the dartboard's bull's-eye.

"Unbelievable!" said the incredulous bartender. True to his word, he prepared a martini and set it before the guy. He then laid a beautiful long-stemmed rose on the bar next to the cocktail.

"What's this?" asked the drunk.

"That's our special prize for being so good at darts," said the bartender.

"Oh," said the drunk. "All out of roast beef on a hard roll, huh?"

Sam was throwing back a few beers at a busy local bar when he glanced over and noticed a drunk passed out at a nearby table. The bartender told him the drunk was Mr. Michaels, and he asked Sam if he could drive Mr. Michaels home. Being a good-hearted sort, Sam agreed. The bartender wrote down Mr. Michaels's address for Sam and returned to his other customers.

Sam went over to Mr. Michaels and tried to rouse him, but he was very groggy and very drunk. Sam helped Mr. Michaels to his feet, but he fell to the floor in a heap.

Good lord, Sam thought. How could anyone drink so much? He took Mr. Michaels by the arm and practically dragged him out to the car. He propped him up against the side of the car while he fumbled for his keys, but Mr. Michaels immediately slid to the ground. Sam found his keys and somehow managed to get Mr. Michaels into the car. They drove to the address the bartender had given Sam.

When they arrived, Sam opened the passenger door and helped Mr. Michaels out of the car. Again, he fell promptly to the ground in a heap. Sam managed to drag him to the front door and help him to his feet.

Just then, Mrs. Michaels appeared at the door.

"You must be Mrs. Michaels," Sam said. "Your husband had a little too much to drink tonight, so I gave him a ride home."

"Oh, that was so nice of you," Mrs. Michaels said, looking around. "But where is his wheelchair?"

One night a man walks into a bar with a pig. The bartender, being the observant sort, notices right off that the pig has a wooden leg. He goes over to the man and asks about it.

The man says, "For a beer I'll tell you all about this very special pig."

The bartender figures it's got to be a good story, and so he gives the man a beer.

The man begins, "Let me tell you about this pig. He is one special pig. One night, about a year ago, my house caught fire. This pig broke out of his pen, woke me and my wife, and then guided us out of the house. This pig saved my life and my family's lives."

The bartender, impressed but still wondering about the leg, says, "Well, that's great. But why does he have a wooden leg?"

The man says, "For another beer I'll tell you about this very special pig."

The bartender, hooked, gives him another beer.

The man says, "Out behind my house there is a small lake. I was out sailing on it when the boat capsized. I cracked my head on the boom and couldn't swim. This pig broke out of his pen, swam out to me, and dragged me to the shore. He then went into the house and got my wife to come out. She gave me mouth-to-mouth resuscitation. This pig saved my life."

The bartender, fascinated but getting a little impatient, says, "That's really terrific, but why the wooden leg?"

The man says, "For another beer—"

The bartender gives him another beer.

The man says, "Let me tell you about this pig. He is one special pig. Last week during a tornado I was on my way to the basement when I stepped on a rake and knocked myself out. This pig broke out of his pen and dragged me into the basement. He saved my life."

The bartender, figuring this has got to be the last story, says, "Wow, that is one special pig. He saved you from a fire, from a tornado, and from drowning. But why does he have a wooden leg?"

The man says, "Well, sir, with a pig this special, you don't eat it all at once."

A man spent a long evening tossing down quite a few beers in a local bar. Just after midnight, he finally staggered out into the cold, wet night to find his way home. It was raining so hard that, combined with his condition, he couldn't see very well and he got lost. He found himself in the town's cemetery not far from the bar. The rain got even worse, and he suddenly slipped and tumbled into a freshly dug grave. The rain, the mud, and all the beer overcame him, and he couldn't climb out. "Help!" he cried instead. "Help! I'm so cold!"

A little while later, another highly inebriated patron left the bar. As luck would have it, the second man was soon near enough to the cemetery to hear the first drunk's cries.

"Help! I'm so cold! I'm so cold!" the cries continued.

The second drunk followed the voice and approached the grave. As he peered over the side, the first drunk looked up and yelled again, "Help! I'm so cold!"

"Of course you're cold," replied the second drunk. "You've kicked off all your dirt."

A man was waiting for his wife to give birth.

The doctor came in and informed the dad that his son had been born without torso, arms, or legs: The son was nothing more than a head.

But the dad grew to love his son, and he raised him as well as he could, with love and compassion.

After twenty-one years, the son was old enough for his first drink. Dad took him to the bar and tearfully told the son he was proud of him. Dad ordered up the biggest, strongest drink for his boy. With all the bar patrons looking on curiously, and the bartender shaking his head in disbelief, the boy took his first sip of alcohol. *Swoooop!* A torso popped out from under the boy's head!

The bar was dead silent, then burst into whoops of joy.

The father, shocked, begged his son to drink again.

The patrons chanted, "Take another drink!"

The bartender still shook his head in dismay.

Then—*swoooop!* Two arms popped out. The bar went wild.

The father, crying and wailing, begged his son to drink again. The patrons chanted "Take another drink!" The bartender ignored the whole affair.

By that point, the boy was getting tipsy, and with his new hands he reached down, grabbed his drink, and guzzled the last of it. *Swoooop!* Two legs popped out.

The bar was in chaos. The father thanked God. The boy stood up on his new legs and stumbled to the left . . . then to the right . . . and through the front door and onto the street, where a truck ran into him and killed him instantly.

The bar fell silent. The father moaned in grief. The bartender cleaned his glasses and whistled an old Irish tune. The father looked at the bartender in disbelief and asked, "How can you be so cold? So callous?"

The bartender said, "That boy should have quit while he was a head."

A man got pulled over by a cop because he was weaving in and out of the lanes. The cop got out of his car and asked the driver to blow into a breath-analyzer tube so the cop could check his alcohol level.

The driver replied, "Oh, no, Officer, I can't do that. I have really bad asthma, and if I do that I'll have an asthma attack and I'll probably die."

"Okay," said the officer, "let's go down to the station and you can urinate into a cup to check your alcohol level."

The driver protested again. "Oh, no, I can't do that either, Officer, because I'm a diabetic, and if I urinate, my blood sugar level will go down so low that I might die."

"Fine then," said the officer again. "Let's go to the station and take a blood test to check your alcohol level."

"Oh, I can't do that either," said the driver. "I'm a hemophiliac and I'll never stop bleeding if you draw blood from me."

In a final attempt, the officer said, "All right then, just step outside your car and walk this white line for me."

"Oh, I can't do that either," the driver said again.

"And why not?" asked the officer.

"Because I'm drunk," said the driver.

A fellow decided to take off early from work and go drinking. He stayed in the bar until it closed at two A.M., by which time he was extremely drunk.

When he entered his house, he didn't want to wake anyone, so he took off his shoes and tiptoed up the stairs. Halfway up the stairs, he fell over backward and landed flat on his rear end. That wouldn't have been so bad, except that he had a couple of empty pint bottles in his back pockets. When they shattered, the broken glass carved up his buttocks terribly. But he was so drunk he didn't know he was hurt.

A few minutes later, as he was undressing, he noticed blood, so he checked himself out in the mirror. Sure enough, his behind was cut up something terrible. Well, he repaired the damage as best as he could under the circumstances, and he went to bed.

The next morning, his head was hurting, and his rear was hurting, and he was hunkering under the covers trying to think up some good story when his wife came into the bedroom.

"Well, you really tied one on last night," she said. "Where'd you go?"

"I worked late," he said, "and I stopped off for a couple of beers."

"A couple of beers? That's a laugh," she replied. "You got plastered last night. Where the heck did you go?"

"What makes you so sure I got drunk last night, anyway?"

"Well," she replied, "my first big clue was when I got up this morning and found a bunch of Band-Aids stuck to the mirror."

Signs That You Are Drinking Too Much

You lose arguments with inanimate objects.

Your doctor finds traces of blood in your alcohol stream.

Your career won't progress beyond senator from Massachusetts.

You sincerely believe alcohol to be the elusive fifth food group.

That damned pink elephant followed you home again.

The parking lot seems to have moved while you were in the bar.

Every woman you see has an exact twin.

You discover in the morning that your liquid cleaning supplies have mysteriously disappeared.

Five beers have just as many calories as a burger, so you skip dinner.

The glass keeps missing your mouth.

When you go to donate blood, they ask what proof it is.

Mosquitoes and vampires catch a buzz after biting you.

You believe your only drinking problem is not having a drink right now.

Your idea of cutting back is less seltzer.

You wake up in the bedroom still clothed, but your underwear is in the bathroom.

Even rednecks have stopped doing jokes about your drinking.

An Irishman walked into a bar in Dublin, ordered three pints of Guinness, and sat in the back of the room, drinking a sip out of each pint in turn. When he finished them, he returned to the bar and ordered three more.

The bartender asked him, "You know, a pint goes flat pretty quickly after I draw it; it would taste better if you bought one at a time."

The Irishman replied, "Well, you see, I have two brothers. One is in America, the other in Australia, and I'm here in Dublin. When we all left home, we promised that we'd drink this way to remember the days we all drank together."

The bartender admitted that this was a nice custom and left it at that.

The Irishman became a regular in the bar and always drank the same way: He ordered three pints and drank them in turn.

One day, he came in and ordered two pints.

All the other regulars in the bar noticed and fell silent. When he came back to the bar for the second round, the bartender said, "I don't want to intrude on your grief, but I wanted to offer my condolences on your great loss."

The Irishman looked confused for a moment; then a light dawned in his eyes, and he laughed. "Oh, no," he said, "Everyone is fine. I've just quit drinking!"

A guy goes into a bar, orders twelve shots, and starts drinking them as fast as he can. The bartender says, "Why are you drinking so fast?"

The guy says, "You'd be drinking fast if you had what I have."

The bartender says, "What do you have?"

The guy says, "Seventy-five cents."

The Battle of the Sexes

A man and a woman who have never met before find themselves in the same sleeping carriage of a train. After the initial embarrassment, they both manage to get to sleep, the woman on the top bunk, the man on the lower.

In the middle of the night the woman leans over and says, "I'm sorry to bother you, but I'm awfully cold and I was wondering if you could possibly pass me another blanket."

The man leans out and, with a glint in his eye, says, "I've got a better idea . . . let's pretend we're married."

"Why not." The woman giggles.

"Good," he replies. "Get your own damn blanket."

When Irving retired, he and his wife, who was much younger, moved to Boca Raton. Once they'd settled in, he decided it was about time to make a will, so he made an appointment with a lawyer.

"It's nice and straightforward," he instructed the attorney. "Everything goes to Rachel—the house, the car, the pension, the life insurance—under the condition that she remarry within the year."

"Fine, Mr. Patron," said the lawyer. "But do you mind my asking why the condition?"

"Simple: I want at least one person to be sorry I died."

A guy runs all the way home and bursts in, yelling to his wife, "Pack your bags, I just won the lottery!"

She says, "Oh, wonderful! Should I pack for the beach or the mountains?"

He replies, "I don't care. . . . Just get the hell out!"

One fine autumn day, Sam was out raking leaves when he noticed a hearse slowly drive by. Following the first hearse was a second hearse, which was followed by a man walking solemnly along, followed by a dog, and then about two hundred men walking in single file.

Intrigued, Sam went up to the man following the second hearse and asked him who was in the first hearse.

"My wife," the man replied.

"I'm sorry," said Sam. "What happened to her?"

"My dog bit her and she died."

Sam then asked the man who was in the second hearse.

The man replied, "My mother-in-law. My dog bit her and she died as well."

Sam thought about this for a while. He finally asked the man, "Can I borrow your dog?"

The man sighed. "Get in line."

A man was sitting quietly reading his paper one morning, peacefully enjoying himself, when his wife sneaked up behind him and clobbered him on the back of his head with a huge cast-iron frying pan.

"What was that for?" the man screamed in pain.

"What is this piece of paper in your pants pocket with the name Marylou written on it?"

"Oh, honey. Don't you remember two weeks ago when I went to the horse races? Marylou was the name of one of the horses I bet on."

The wife seemed satisfied and headed on to do some work around the house, feeling a bit sheepish. Three days later the man was once again sitting in his chair when his wife sneaked up on him and again hit him on the head with a cast-iron frying pan.

"What's that for this time?" the man shouted, clutching his head.

"Your horse called."

Two women were shopping. When they started to discuss their home lives, one said, "Seems like all Alfred and I do anymore is fight. I've been so upset I've lost twenty pounds."

"Why don't you just leave him then?" asked her friend.

"Oh! Not yet," the first replied. "I'd like to lose at least another ten to fifteen pounds first."

The Fundamental Differences Between the Sexes:

A man will pay $2 for a $1 item he wants.
A woman will pay $1 for a $2 item she doesn't want.

A woman worries about the future until she gets a husband.
A man never worries about the future until he gets a wife.

A successful man is one who makes more money than his wife can spend.
A successful woman is one who can find such a man.

To be happy with a man you must understand him a lot and love him a little.
To be happy with a woman you must love her a lot and not try to understand her at all.

Married men live longer than single men, but married men are a lot more willing to die.

Any married man should forget his mistakes—there's no use in two people remembering the same thing.

Men wake up as good looking as they were when they went to bed.
Women somehow deteriorate during the night.

A woman marries a man expecting he will change, but he doesn't.

A man marries a woman expecting that she won't change, and she does.

A woman has the last word in any argument. Anything a man says after that is the beginning of a new argument.

There are two times when a man doesn't understand a woman—before marriage and after marriage.

Reasons It's Great to Be a Guy

Phone conversations are over in thirty seconds flat.

When clicking through the channel, you don't have to stall on every shot of someone crying.

You know stuff about tanks.

A five-day vacation requires only one suitcase.

You don't have to monitor your friends' sex lives.

Your bathroom lines are 80 percent shorter.

You can open all your own jars.

Old friends don't give you crap if you've lost or gained weight.

Dry cleaners and haircutters don't rob you blind.

A beer gut does not make you invisible to the opposite sex.

You don't have to lug a bag of useful stuff around everywhere you go.

You can leave a hotel bed unmade.

When your work is criticized, you don't have to panic that everyone secretly hates you.

The garage is all yours.

You get extra credit for the slightest act of thoughtfulness.

You can be showered and ready in ten minutes.

Wedding plans take care of themselves.

If someone forgets to invite you to something, he or she can still be your friend.

Your underwear costs $10 for a three-pack.

None of your coworkers has the power to make you cry.

You don't have to shave below your neck.

If you're thirty-four and single, nobody notices.

Everything on your face stays its original color.

Chocolate is just another snack.

Flowers fix everything.

Three pairs of shoes are more than enough.

Nobody stops telling a good dirty joke when you walk into the room.

You don't have to clean your apartment if the meter reader is coming by.

Car mechanics tell you the truth.

You don't care whether anybody notices your new haircut.

You can watch a game in silence with your buddy for hours without even thinking, He must be mad at me.

You never misconstrue innocuous statements to mean your lover is about to leave you.

One mood, all the time.

You can admire Clint Eastwood without starving yourself to look like him.

You can sit with your knees apart no matter what you are wearing.

Gray hair and wrinkles add character.

You don't care if someone is talking about you behind your back.

You don't mooch off others' desserts.

If you retain water, it's in a canteen.

The remote is yours and yours alone.

People never glance at your chest when you're talking to them.

You can drop by to see a friend without bringing a little gift.

Bachelor parties have it all over bridal showers.

You have a normal and healthy relationship with your mother.

If you don't call your buddy when you say you will, he won't tell your friends you've changed.

If another guy shows up at the party in the same outfit, you might become lifelong buddies.

You don't have to remember birthdays and anniversaries for everyone you know.

Your pals can be trusted never to trap you with: "So . . . notice anything different?"

There is always a game on somewhere.

The Male vs. Female World of the New Haircut

Women's version:

SUE: Oh! You got a haircut! That's so cute!

ANNE: Do you think so? I wasn't sure when she gave me the mirror. I mean, you don't think it's too fluffy looking?

SUE: Oh, God, no! No, it's perfect. I'd love to get my hair cut like that, but I think my face is too wide. I'm pretty much stuck with this stuff, I think.

ANNE: Are you serious? I think your face is adorable. And you could easily get one of those layer cuts—that would look so cute. I was actually going to do that except I was afraid it would accent my long neck.

SUE: Oh—that's funny! I would love to have your neck! Anything to take attention away from this two-by-four I have for a shoulder line.

ANNE: Are you kidding? I know girls who would love to have your shoulders. Everything drapes so well on you. I mean, look at my arms. See how short they are? If I had your shoulders I could get clothes to fit me so much easier.

Men's version:

BOB: Haircut?

TOM: Yeah.

What Men Really Mean

"I'm going fishing." Really means: "I'm going to drink myself dangerously stupid, then stand by a stream with a stick in my hand while the fish swim by in complete safety."

"Let's take your car." Really means: "Mine is full of beer cans, burger wrappers, and is completely out of gas."

"Woman driver." Really means: "Someone who doesn't speed, tailgate, swear, make obscene gestures, and has a better driving record than me."

"I don't care what color you paint the kitchen." Really means: "As long as it's not blue, green, pink, red, yellow, lavender, gray, mauve, black, turquoise, or any other color besides white."

"It's a guy thing." Really means: "There is no rational thought pattern connected with it, and you have no chance at all of making it logical."

"Can I help with dinner?" Really means: "Why isn't it already on the table?"

"Uh-huh," "Sure, honey," or "Yes, dear." Really mean:

Absolutely nothing. It's a conditioned response like Pavlov's dog drooling.

"Good idea." Really means: "It'll never work. And I'll spend the rest of the day gloating."

"Have you lost weight?" Really means: "I've just spent our last thirty dollars on a cordless drill."

"My wife doesn't understand me." Really means: "She's heard all my stories before and is tired of them."

"It would take too long to explain." Really means: "I have no idea how it works."

"I'm getting more exercise lately." Really means: "The batteries in the remote are dead."

"I got a lot done." Really means: "I found Waldo in almost every picture."

"We're going to be late." Really means: "Now I have a legitimate excuse to drive like a maniac."

"Hey, I've read all the classics." Really means: "I've been subscribing to *Playboy* since 1972."

"You cook just like my mother used to." Really means: "She used the smoke detector as a meal timer, too."

"I was listening to you. It's just that I have things on my mind." Really means: "I was wondering if that redhead over there is wearing a bra."

"Take a break, honey, you're working too hard." Really means: "I can't hear the game over the vacuum cleaner."

"That's interesting, dear." Really means: "Are you still talking?"

"Honey, we don't need material things to prove our love." Really means: "I forgot our anniversary again."

"You expect too much of me." Really means: "You want me to stay awake."

"It's a really good movie." Really means: "It's got guns, knives, fast cars, and Heather Locklear."

"That's women's work." Really means: "It's difficult, dirty, and thankless."

"Will you marry me?" Really means: "Both my roommates have moved out, I can't find the washer, and there is no more peanut butter."

"Go ask your mother." Really means: "I am incapable of making a decision."

"You know how bad my memory is." Really means: "I remember the theme song to *F Troop*, the address of the first girl I ever kissed, and the Vehicle Identification Numbers of every car I've ever owned, but I forgot your birthday."

"I was just thinking about you, and I got you these roses." Really means: "The girl selling them on the corner was a real babe."

"Football is a man's game." Really means: "Women are generally too smart to play it."

"Oh, don't fuss. I just cut myself, it's no big deal." Really means: "I have actually severed a limb, but I will bleed to death before I admit I'm hurt."

"I do help around the house." Really means: "I once put a dirty towel in the laundry basket."

"Hey, I've got my reasons for what I'm doing." Really means: "And I sure hope I think of some pretty soon."

"I can't find it." Really means: "It didn't fall into my outstretched hands, so I'm completely clueless."

"What did I do this time?" Really means: "What did you catch me at?"

"What do you mean, you need new clothes?" Really means: "You just bought new clothes three years ago."

"She's one of those rabid feminists." Really means: "She refused to make my coffee."

"But I hate to go shopping." Really means: "Because I always wind up outside the dressing room holding your purse."

"No, I left plenty of gas in the car." Really means: "You may actually get it to start."

"I'm going to stop off for a quick one with the guys." Really means: "I am planning on drinking myself into a vegetative stupor with my chest-pounding, mouth-breathing, preevolutionary companions."

"I heard you." Really means: "I haven't the foggiest clue what you said and am hoping desperately that I can fake it well enough so that you don't spend the next three days yelling at me."

"You know I could never love anyone else." Really means: "I am used to the way you yell at me, and I realize it could be worse."

"You look terrific." Really means: "Oh, God, please don't try on one more outfit. I'm starving."

"I brought you a present." Really means: "It was free ice scraper night at the ball game."

"I missed you." Really means: "I can't find my sock drawer, the kids are hungry, and we are out of toilet paper."

"I'm not lost. I know exactly where we are." Really means: "No one will see us alive ever again."

"We share the housework." Really means: "I make the messes, she cleans them up."

"This relationship is getting too serious." Really means: "I like you more than my truck."

"I recycle." Really means: "We could pay the rent with the money from my empties."

"Of course I like it, honey, you look beautiful." Really means: "Oh, man, what have you done to yourself?"

"It sure snowed last night." Really means: "I suppose you're going to nag me about shoveling the walk now."

"It's good beer." Really means: "It was on sale."

"I don't need to read the instructions." Really means: "I am perfectly capable of screwing it up without printed help."

"I'll fix the garbage disposal later." Really means: "If I wait long enough you'll get frustrated and buy a new one."

"I broke up with her." Really means: "She dumped me."

"I'll take you to a fancy restaurant." Really means: "Someplace that doesn't have a drive-through window."

How Dogs and Men Are the Same:

Both take up too much space on the bed.

Both have irrational fears about vacuum cleaning.

Both are threatened by their own kind.

Both mark their territory.

The smaller ones tend to be more nervous.

Neither does any dishes.

Neither of them notices when you get your hair cut.

Both are suspicious of the postman.

Neither understands what you see in cats.

The guy called up his lawyer to tell him he was suing for divorce, and the lawyer inquired as to his grounds for the suit.

"Can you believe my wife says I'm a lousy lover?" sputtered the husband.

"*That's* why you're suing?" asked the lawyer.

"Of course not. I'm suing because she knows the difference."

Male Bashing

Why are blonde jokes so short?

So men can understand them.

How do some men define Roe vs. Wade?

Two ways to cross a river.

What do you call a woman who knows where her husband is every night?

A widow.

Man said to God: "God, why did you make woman so beautiful?"

God replied, "So you would love her."

"But God," the man says, "why did you make her so dumb?"

God said: "So she would love you."

What is the difference between a wife and a girlfriend?

Forty-five pounds.

And what is the difference between a husband and a boyfriend?

Forty-five minutes.

A painfully shy guy went into a bar and saw a beautiful woman sitting at the bar. After an hour of gathering up his courage, he finally went over to her and asked tentatively, "Um, would you mind if I chatted with you for a while?"

She responded by yelling, at the top of her lungs, "No, I won't sleep with you tonight!"

Everyone in the bar was now staring at them. Naturally, the guy was hopelessly and completely embarrassed and he slunk back to his table.

After a few minutes, the woman walked over to him and apologized. She smiled at him and explained, "I'm sorry if I embarrassed you. You see, I'm a graduate student in psychology and I'm studying how people respond to embarrassing situations."

To which he responded, at the top of his lungs, "What do you mean, two hundred dollars?"

Two men were having a drink in a London pub at lunchtime. After conversing for a while, one said to the other, "I had a terribly embarrassing experience last evening. I went up to the ticket window, meaning to purchase a ticket to Piccadilly, and instead I asked for a ticket to Tickadilly!"

"I know just what you mean," replied the other chap. "Only this morning at breakfast I meant to ask my wife to please pass the butter. Instead, to my acute embarrassment, I said, 'You hopeless bitch, you ruined my life.' "

Women's Grasp of English:

Yes = No

No = Yes

Maybe = No

I'm sorry. = You'll be sorry.

We need. = I want.

It's your decision. = The correct decision should be obvious by now.

Do what you want. = You'll pay for this later.

We need to talk. = I need to complain.

Sure, go ahead. = I don't want you to.

I'm not upset. = Of course I'm upset, you moron!

You're . . . so manly. = You need a shave and a new deodorant.

You're certainly attractive tonight. = Is sex all you ever think about?

Be romantic, turn out the lights. = I have flabby thighs.

This kitchen is so inconvenient. = I want a new house.

I want new curtains. = And carpeting, and furniture, and wallpaper . . .

I heard a noise. = I noticed you were almost asleep.

Do you love me? = I'm going to ask for something expensive.

How much do you love me? = I did something today you're really not going to like.

I'll be ready in a minute. = Kick off your shoes and find a good game on TV.

Is my butt fat? = Tell me I'm beautiful.

You have to learn to communicate. = Just agree with me.

Are you listening to me!? = Too late, you're dead.

Was that the baby? = Get out of bed and walk him until he goes to sleep.

I'm not yelling! = Yes, I am yelling, because I think this is important.

Men's Grasp of English

I'm hungry. = I'm hungry.

I'm sleepy. = I'm sleepy.

I'm tired. = I'm tired.

Do you want to go to a movie? = I'd eventually like to have sex with you.

Can I take you out to dinner? = I'd eventually like to have sex with you.

Can I call you sometime? = I'd eventually like to have sex with you.

May I have this dance? = I'd eventually like to have sex with you.

Nice dress! = Nice body!

You look tense; let me give you a massage. = I want to fondle you.

What's wrong? = I don't see why you are making such a big deal out of this.

What's wrong? = What meaningless self-inflicted trauma are you going through now?

What's wrong? = I guess sex tonight is out of the question.

I'm bored. = Do you want to have sex?

I love you. = Let's have sex now.

I love you, too. = Okay, I said it . . . we'd better have sex now!

Yes, I like the way you cut your hair. = I liked it better before.

Yes, I like the way you cut your hair. = Fifty bucks and it doesn't even look different!

Let's talk. = I am trying to impress you by showing that I am a deep person and maybe then you'd like to have sex with me.

Will you marry me? = I want to make it illegal for you to have sex with other guys.

(While shopping) I like that one better. = Pick any freakin' dress and let's go home!

Attending a wedding for the first time, a little girl whispered to her mother, "Why is the bride dressed in white?"

"Because white is the color of happiness, and today is the happiest day of her life," her mother tried to explain, keeping it simple.

The child thought about this for a moment, then said, "So why's the groom wearing black?"

During the wedding rehearsal, the groom approached the pastor with an unusual offer.

"Look, I'll give you one hundred dollars if you'll change the wedding vows. When you get to me and the part where I'm to promise to 'love, honor, and obey' and 'forsaking all others, be faithful to her forever,' I'd appreciate it if you'd just leave that part out." He passed the minister a one-hundred-dollar bill and walked away, relieved.

The day of the wedding came, and so did that part of the ceremony where the bride and groom exchange vows. When it came time for the groom's vows, the pastor looked the young man in the eye and said: "Will you promise to prostrate yourself before her, obey her every command and wish, serve her breakfast in bed every morning of your life, and swear eternally before God and your lovely wife that you will not ever even look at another woman, as long as you both shall live?"

The groom gulped, looked around, and said in a tiny voice, "I do." Then the groom leaned toward the pastor and hissed, "I thought we had a deal!"

The pastor put the one-hundred-dollar bill back into the groom's hand and whispered, "She made me a much better offer."

Marriage Jokes, Some New and Some Real Chestnuts:

Marriage is not a word. It is a sentence (a life sentence!).

Marriage is very much like a violin; after the sweet music is over, the strings are attached.

Marriage is love. Love is blind. Therefore marriage is an institution for the blind.

Marriage is a thing that puts a ring on a woman's finger and two under the man's eyes.

Marriage certificate is just another term for a work permit.

Marriage requires a man to prepare four types of "rings": the engagement ring, the wedding ring, the suffe-ring, the endu-ring.

Married life is full of excitement and frustration: In the first year of marriage, the man speaks and the woman listens. In the second year, the woman speaks and the man listens. In the third year, they *both* speak and the *neighbors* listen.

It is true that love is blind, but marriage is definitely an eye-opener.

Getting married is very much like going to a restaurant with friends. You order what you want, and when you see what the other fellow has, you wish you had ordered that.

It's true that all men are born free and equal, but some of them get *married*!

There once was a man who muttered a few words in the church and found himself married. A year later he muttered something in his sleep and found himself divorced.

A happy marriage is a matter of giving and taking; the husband gives and the wife takes.

SON: How much does it cost to get married, Dad?

FATHER: I don't know son, I'm still paying for it.

SON: Is it true? Dad, I heard that in ancient China, a man doesn't know his wife until he marries.

FATHER: That happens everywhere, son, *everywhere*!

There was a man who said, "I never knew what happiness was until I got married . . . and then it was too late!"

Love is one long sweet dream, and marriage is the alarm clock.

They say that when a man holds a woman's hand before marriage, it is love; after marriage, it is self-defense.

When a newly married man looks happy, we know why. But when a ten-year married man looks happy, we wonder why.

There was this lover who said that he would go through hell for her. They got married, and now he *is* going through hell.

One night a wife found her husband standing over their newborn baby's crib. Silently she watched him. As he stood looking down at the sleeping infant, she saw on his face a mixture of emotions: disbelief, doubt, delight, amazement, enchantment, skepticism.

Touched by this unusual display and the deep emotions it aroused, with eyes glistening she slipped her arms around her husband.

"A penny for your thoughts," she whispered in his ear.

"It's amazing!" he replied. "I just can't see how anybody can make a crib like that for only $46.50!"

A couple was invited to a swanky masked Halloween party.

The evening of the event, the woman got a terrible headache and told her husband to go to the party without her. Being a devoted husband, he protested, but she argued that she was simply going to take some aspirin and go to bed, and that there was no need for his good time to be spoiled by staying home. So he reluctantly took his costume and away he went.

The wife, after sleeping soundly for one hour, awakened without a headache. As it was still early, she decided to go the party after all. And because her husband did not know what her costume was, she thought she would have some fun by watching her husband to see how he acted when she was not with him.

She joined the party and soon spotted her husband cavorting around on the dance floor, dancing with every woman he could, and trying, with some success, to get in a kiss here and there. His wife sidled up to him and behaved in an openly seductive manner. He quickly lost interest in the others, especially because she let him go as far as he wished; after all, he was her husband. It wasn't long before he whispered a proposition in her ear. She agreed, and off they went behind a locked door.

Just before the unmasking at midnight, she slipped away and rushed home, put the costume away, and got into bed, wondering what kind of explanation he would make for his behavior.

She was sitting up reading when he came in, and she asked what kind of a time he had. He said, "Oh, the same old thing. You know I never have a good time when you're not there."

Then she asked, "Did you dance much?"

He replied, "I didn't even dance one dance. When I got there, I met Pete, Bill Brown, and some other guys, so we went into the den and played poker all evening. But you're not going to believe what happened to the guy I loaned my costume to. . . ."

Men are like a fine wine. They all start out like grapes, and you have to stomp on them and keep them in the dark until they mature into something you'd like to have dinner with.

Why a Beer Is Better than a Man

A beer NEVER leaves the toilet seat up.

A beer won't expect you to cook dinner when you're not hungry.

A beer doesn't care if you go shopping.

A beer doesn't mind when your mother visits.

A beer does as many chores as a man, with a LOT less complaining.

A beer won't tease you because you once liked Barry Manilow.

If a beer had a sports car, it wouldn't love it more than you.

A beer doesn't want to go out alone with the other beers.

A beer doesn't sulk.

A beer doesn't have to sleep with the windows open.

A beer doesn't snore.

A beer can't interrupt.

A beer doesn't care that you can't find your car's carburetor.

A beer doesn't care that you don't balance your checkbook.

A good beer is easy to find.

A beer doesn't have friends who will drink your beer.

A beer wouldn't yell if you dented the car.

A beer won't get jealous if you enjoy another beer.

A beer won't care if you gain five pounds.

A beer doesn't want children.

If the beer is finished before you are, you can have another beer.

Hangovers go away.

A beer will never invite friends home for dinner without calling.

A beer's life does not revolve around football.

A beer would never make fun of your new outfit.

A beer never needs a shave.

A beer doesn't care what toppings you get on the pizza.

Just because you have dinner with a beer doesn't mean you have to sleep with a beer.

A beer doesn't have morning breath.

A beer is happy to go wherever you want to go.

A beer will never drink the last beer.

A beer will never take the newspaper apart before you've read it.

A beer will never worry about losing its hair.

A beer won't steal the covers.

You don't have to laugh at a beer's jokes.

A wife asked her husband, "Honey, if I died, would you remarry?"

"After a considerable period of grieving, I guess I would. We all need companionship."

"If I died and you remarried," the wife asked, "would she live in this house?"

"We've spent a lot of money getting this house just

the way we want it. I'm not going to get rid of my house. I guess she would, yes."

"If I died and you remarried and she lived in this house," the wife continued, "would she sleep in our bed?"

"Well, the bed is brand new, and it cost us over two thousand dollars. It's going to last a long time, so I guess she would."

"If I died and you remarried and she lived in this house and slept in our bed, would she use my golf clubs?"

"Oh, no," the husband replied. "She's left-handed."

A passenger plane on a cross-country trip encountered a terrible storm. The plane got pounded by rain, hail, wind, and lightning. The passengers were screaming, certain that the plane was going to crash and that they were all going to die.

At the height of the storm, a young woman jumped up and exclaimed, "I can't take this anymore! I can't just sit here and die like an animal, strapped into a chair. If I am going to die, let me die feeling like a woman. Is there anyone here who's man enough to make me feel like a woman?"

She saw a hand go up in the back of the plane, and an incredibly handsome, tall, muscular man with dark, flowing hair smiled and started to walk up to her seat.

As he approached her, he slowly took off his shirt. She could see his impressive musculature even in the faltering lighting of the plane. He stood in front of her, shirt in hand, and said, "I can make you feel like a woman before you die. Are you interested?"

She eagerly nodded her head. "Yes!"

The man handed her his shirt and said, "Here. Iron this."

A wife and her husband were having a dinner party for some important guests. The wife was very excited about this and wanted everything to be perfect. At the very last minute, she realized that she didn't have any snails for the party, so she asked her husband to run down to the beach with the bucket to gather some fresh ones.

Very grudgingly, he agreed. He took the bucket and walked out the door, down the steps, and out to the beach. As he was collecting the snails, he noticed a beautiful woman strolling alongside the water just a little farther down the beach.

He kept thinking to himself, Wouldn't it be great if she would just come down and talk to me? He went back to gathering the snails. All of a sudden, he looked up, and the beautiful woman was standing right over him. They started talking, and eventually she invited him back to her place. They ended up spending the night together.

At seven o'clock the next morning, he woke up and exclaimed, "Oh, no! My wife's dinner party!"

He gathered all his clothes, struggled into them quickly, grabbed his bucket, and ran out the door. He ran along the beach all the way to his apartment. He ran up the stairs of his apartment. He was in such a hurry that when he got to the top of the stairs, he dropped the bucket of snails, scattering them all the way down the stairs.

Just then, the door opened; his very angry wife stood in the doorway wondering where he'd been all this time.

He looked at the snails all down the steps; then he looked at her, then back at the snails, and he said, "Come on, guys, we're almost there!"

Man: Haven't I seen you someplace before?
Woman: Yes, that's why I don't go there anymore.

Man: Is this seat empty?
Woman: Yes, and this one will be if you sit down.

Man: Your body is like a temple.
Woman: Sorry there are no services today.

Man: I would go to the end of the world for you.
Woman: But would you stay there?

What Women Should Know About Men

If you think the way to a man's heart is through his stomach, you're aiming too high.

Women don't make fools of men—most of them are the do-it-yourself types.

A woman's work that is never done is the stuff she asked her husband to do.

If you want a nice man go for a bald one—they try harder.

Men are all the same—they just have different faces so you can tell them apart.

Whenever you meet a man who would make a good husband, you will usually find that he is.

Scientists have just discovered something that can do the work of five men—a woman.

Men's brains are like the prison system: not enough cells per man.

Husbands are like children: They're fine if they're someone else's.

Never do housework. No man ever made love to a woman because the house was spotless.

Don't imagine you can change a man—unless he's in diapers.

If they put a man on the moon, they should be able to put them all there.

Tell him you're not his type: You have a pulse.

Never let your man's mind wander—it's too little to be let out alone.

Definition of a bachelor: a man who has missed the opportunity to make some woman miserable.

The children of Israel wandered around the desert for forty years. Even in biblical times men wouldn't ask for directions.

If he asks what sort of books you're interested in, tell him checkbooks.

A man's idea of a serious commitment is usually, "Oh, all right, I'll stay the night."

Women sleep with men who, if they were women, they wouldn't even have bothered to have lunch with.

Remember: A sense of humor does not mean that you tell him jokes; it means you laugh at his.

Sadly, all men are created equal.

A man and a woman were married for forty years. When they first got married, the man said, "I am putting a box under the bed. You must promise never to look in it."

In all their forty years of marriage, the woman never looked. However, on the afternoon of their fortieth anniversary, curiosity got the best of her; she lifted the lid and peeked inside. In the box were three empty beer bottles and about $300 in small bills. She closed the box and put it back under the bed. Now that she knew what was in the box, she was doubly curious as to why.

That evening they were out for a special dinner at their favorite restaurant. After dinner the woman could no longer contain her curiosity, and she confessed, saying, "I am so sorry. For all these years I kept my promise and never looked. However, today the temptation was too much, and I gave in. But now I need to know, why do you keep the bottles in the box?"

The man thought for a while and said, "I guess after all these wonderful years, you deserve to know the truth. Whenever I was unfaithful to you, I put an empty beer bottle in the box under the bed to remind myself not to do it again."

The woman was shocked, but said, "I am very disappointed and saddened, but I guess after all those years away from home on the road, temptation does happen, and I guess that three times is not so bad considering the number of years."

They hugged and made their peace.

A little while later the woman asked the man, "Why do you have all that money in the box?"

To which the man answered, "Whenever the box filled with empties, I cashed them in."

Why Dogs Are Better than Women

Dogs love it when your friends come over.

Dogs don't care if you use their shampoo.

Dogs think you sing great.

Dogs don't expect you to call when you are running late. The later you are, the more excited dogs are to see you.

Dogs will forgive you for playing with other dogs.

Dogs don't notice if you call them by another dog's name.

Dogs don't mind if you give their offspring away.

Dogs love red meat.

Dogs can appreciate excessive body hair.

Anyone can get a good-looking dog.

If a dog is gorgeous, other dogs don't hate it.

Dogs like it when you leave lots of things on the floor.

Dogs understand that instincts are better than asking for directions.

Dogs know that all animals smaller than dogs were made to be hunted.

Dogs like beer.

Dogs agree that you have to raise your voice to get your point across.

Dogs don't want to know about every other dog you ever had.

A dog would rather have you buy them a hamburger dinner than a lobster dinner.

You never have to wait for a dog. They're ready to go twenty-four hours a day.

Dogs find you amusing when you're drunk.

Top Five Reasons Why Computers Must Be Male

5. They're heavily dependent on external tools and equipment.
4. They periodically cut you off right when you think you've established a network connection.
3. They'll usually do what you ask them to do, but they won't do more than they have to and they won't think of it on their own.
2. They're typically obsolete within five years and need to be traded in for a new model. Some users,

however, feel they've already invested so much in the damn machine that they're compelled to remain with an underpowered system.

1. They get hot when you turn them on, and that's the only time you have their attention.

Top Five Reasons Why Computers Must Be Female

5. No one but their creator understands their internal logic.

4. Even your smallest mistakes are immediately committed to memory for future reference.

3. The native language used to communicate with other computers is incomprehensible to everyone else.

2. The message "Bad command or filename" is about as informative as "If you don't know why I'm mad at you, then I'm certainly not going to tell you."

1. As soon as you make a commitment to one, you find yourself spending half your paycheck on accessories for it.

A newly married man asked his wife, "Would you have married me if my father hadn't left me a fortune?"

"Honey," the woman replied sweetly, "I'd have married you *no matter who left you a fortune.*"

This guy walks into a supermarket and loads up his cart with one bar of soap, one toothbrush, one tube of toothpaste, one pint of milk, and a frozen TV dinner, serving size: one.

At the checkout counter, the checkout girl takes one look at the guy and says, "I bet you're single."

The guy says, "How can you tell?"

The girl says, "Cuz you're ugly."

The Ages of Men and Women

THE MALE STAGES OF LIFE

AGE	DRINK
17	beer
25	bourbon
35	vodka
48	double vodka
66	Maalox

AGE	SEDUCTION LINE
17	My parents are away for the weekend.
25	My girlfriend is away for the weekend.
35	My fiancée is away for the weekend.
48	My wife is away for the weekend.
66	My second wife is dead.

AGE	FAVORITE SPORT
17	sex
25	sex
35	sex
48	sex
66	napping

AGE	DEFINITION OF A SUCCESSFUL DATE
17	tongue
25	breakfast
35	didn't set back my therapy
48	didn't have to meet her kids
66	got home alive

AGE	FAVORITE FANTASY
17	getting to third
25	airplane sex
35	ménage à trois
48	taking the company public
66	Swiss maid/Nazi love slave

AGE	IDEAL AGE TO GET MARRIED
17	25
25	35
35	48
48	66
66	17

AGE	IDEAL DATE
17	triple Stephen King feature at a drive-in
25	split the check before going back to my place
35	just come over
48	just come over and cook
66	sex in the company jet on the way to Vegas

THE FEMALE STAGES OF LIFE

AGE	DRINK
17	wine cooler
25	white wine
35	red wine
48	Dom Perignon
66	shot of Jack with an Ensure chaser

AGE	EXCUSES FOR REFUSING DATES
17	need to wash my hair
25	need to wash and condition my hair
35	need to color my hair
48	need to have Francois color my hair
66	need to have Francois color my wig

AGE	FAVORITE SPORT
17	shopping
25	shopping
35	shopping
48	shopping
66	shopping

AGE	DEFINITION OF A SUCCESSFUL DATE
17	Burger King
25	free meal
35	a diamond
48	a bigger diamond
66	home alone

AGE	FAVORITE FANTASY
17	tall, dark, and handsome man
25	tall, dark, and handsome man with money
35	tall, dark, and handsome man with money and a brain
48	a man with hair
66	a man

AGE	IDEAL AGE TO GET MARRIED
17	17
25	25
35	35
48	48
66	66

AGE	IDEAL DATE
17	He offers to pay.
25	He pays.
35	He cooks breakfast the next morning.
48	He cooks breakfast the next morning for the kids.
66	He can chew breakfast.

There are three guys talking in a pub. Two of them are talking about the amount of control they have over their wives; the third remains quiet.

After a while, one of the first two turns to the third and says, "Well, what about you? What sort of control do you have over your wife?"

The third fellow says, "I'll tell you. Just the other night, my wife came to me on her hands and knees."

The first two guys were amazed! "What happened then?" they asked.

"She said, 'Get out from under the bed and fight like a man!' "

Blondes

Once upon a time, a blonde went to get her hair cut, but she was wearing headphones. The stylist said, "You gotta take off your headphones, or I can't cut your hair."

The blonde said, "No! I can't! I'll just *die* without them!"

So the stylist just sighed and trimmed the ends of her hair until the blonde fell asleep. The stylist said to herself, "I'll just take these off her to cut her hair. She won't notice." So the stylist did just that.

After about three minutes, the blonde fell out of the chair, dead.

The stylist said, "I wonder what could have possibly killed her? Maybe it had something to do with the headphones after all."

She took the blonde's headphones and put them on her own head, just to see what was playing. On the headphones, a voice repeated, "Breathe in, breathe out."

There was a blonde who was sick and tired of being ridiculed for being blonde, so she decided to fix it by dyeing her hair brown.

The next day, she was driving along a country road when she saw a shepherd with his flock. She decided to see if she could pass as a brunette and if she had indeed gotten any smarter. She pulled over to the side of the road and asked the shepherd, "If I can guess how many sheep you have, could I have one?"

The shepherd thought this was an unusual request, but he agreed.

The blonde thought about it for a minute and said, "One hundred and fifty." The shepherd said she was right and told her she could pick a sheep to take home.

She did, and as she was putting it into the trunk of the car, the shepherd stopped her and said, "If I can guess your real hair color, can I have my dog back?"

Three women are about to be executed. One's a brunette, one's a redhead, and one's a blonde.

The guard brings the brunette forward, and the executioner asks if she has any last requests. She says no, and the executioner shouts, "Ready! Aim!"

Suddenly the brunette yells, "Earthquake!"

Everyone is startled and looks around. In all the confusion, the brunette escapes.

The guard brings the redhead forward, and the executioner asks if she has any last requests. She says no, and the executioner shouts, "Ready! Aim!"

Suddenly the redhead yells, "Tornado!"

Everyone is startled and looks around, and the redhead escapes.

By now the blonde has it all figured out. The guard brings her forward, and the executioner asks if she has any last requests. She says no, and the executioner shouts, "Ready! Aim!"

And the blonde yells, "Fire!"

Jill, a blonde, approaches the edge of a river. On the other side, she sees another blonde. Jill asks her, "How do I get to the other side of the river?"

The blonde responds, "You're *on* the other side."

A young blonde woman is distraught because she fears her husband is having an affair, so she goes to a gun shop and buys a handgun.

The next day she comes home to find her husband in bed with a beautiful redhead. She grabs the gun and holds it to her own head. The husband jumps out of bed, begging and pleading with her not to shoot herself. Hysterically, the blonde responds to the husband, "Shut up! You're next!"

Hear about the blonde who got an A.M. radio?

It took her a month to realize she could play it at night.

Why did the blonde scale the chain-link fence?

To see what was on the other side.

How do you make a blonde laugh on Saturday?

Tell her a joke on Wednesday.

A brunette who really hated blondes was walking through the desert when she came across a magic lamp. After rubbing the lamp, the genie told her that she got three wishes with one catch: All the blondes in the world would get twice whatever she asked for.

So the brunette thought awhile and then wished for a million dollars.

"Every blonde in the world will get two million," said the genie.

The brunette said that was fine, and then she asked for an incredibly handsome man.

"Every blonde in the world will get two incredibly handsome men," the genie reminded her.

The brunette said that was fine too, and the genie granted her wishes. "Now for your third wish," said the genie.

"See that stick over there?" asked the brunette. "I want you to beat me half to death with it."

A young woman went to a doctor and told him, "You have to help me. I hurt all over."

"What do you mean?" asked the doctor.

The woman touched her right knee with her index finger and yelled, "Ow! That hurts." Then she touched her left cheek and again yelled, "Ouch! That hurts, too." Then she touched her right earlobe. "Ow, even *that* hurts."

The doctor asked the woman, "Are you a natural blonde?"

"Why, yes," she said.

"I thought so," said the doctor. "You have a sprained finger."

What do you do if a blonde throws a pin at you?
Run like hell, she's got the grenade in her mouth!

This guy was driving in a car with a blonde. He told her to stick her head out the window to see if the blinker was working. She stuck her head out and said, "Yes, no, yes, no, yes, no. . . ."

A blonde and a redhead met in a bar after work for a drink, and were watching the six o'clock news. A man was shown threatening to jump from the Brooklyn Bridge.

The blonde bet the redhead $50 that the guy wouldn't jump, and the redhead replied, "I'll take that bet!"

The man jumped, so the blonde gave the redhead the $50.

The redhead said, "I can't take this, you're my friend."

The blonde said, "No, a bet's a bet."

So the redhead said, "Listen, I have to admit, I saw this story on the five o'clock news, so I really can't take your money."

The blonde replied, "Well, so did I, but I never thought he'd jump again!"

Why don't blondes ever double recipes?

The oven temperature doesn't go up to 700 degrees.

A lawyer and a blonde were seated next to each other on a long flight from L.A. to New York City.

The lawyer leaned over and asked if she would like to play a fun game.

The blonde just wanted to take a nap, so she politely declined and leaned over toward the window to catch a few winks.

The lawyer persisted and explained that the game was really easy and a lot of fun. He said, "I ask you questions, and if you don't know the answer, you pay me, and vice versa."

Again she politely declined and tried to get some sleep.

But the lawyer kept at her. "Okay, if you don't know the answer, you pay me five dollars, and if I don't know the answer, I'll pay you fifty dollars," figuring that since she was a blonde he would easily win the match.

This caught the blonde's attention, and, figuring that there would be no end to this torment until she played, she agreed to the game.

The lawyer asked the first question. "What's the distance from the Earth to the moon?"

The blonde didn't say a word. She simply reached into her purse, pulled out a five-dollar bill, and handed it to the lawyer.

Then it was the blonde's turn. She asked the lawyer, "What goes up a hill with three legs and comes down with four?"

The lawyer looked at her with a puzzled expression. He took out his laptop computer and searched all his references. He tapped into the air phone with his modem and searched the Internet and the Library of Congress. Frustrated, he sent E-mails to all his coworkers and friends—all to no avail.

After well over an hour, he awoke the blonde and handed her $50. The blonde politely took the $50, then turned away to go back to sleep.

The lawyer, who was more than a little miffed, tapped the blonde on the shoulder and asked, "Well, so what *is* the answer?"

Without a word, the blonde reached into her purse and handed the lawyer a five-dollar bill. She went back to sleep.

Why did the blonde quit her job as a rest-room attendant?

She couldn't figure out how to refill the hand dryer.

How can you tell if a blonde has been using your lawn mower?

The green WELCOME mat is ripped all to shreds.

What's the advantage of being married to a blonde?

You can park in handicapped zones.

How can you tell which tricycle belongs to the blonde?

It is the one with the kickstand.

What do you call an all-blond skydiving team?

A new version of the lawn darts game.

Why did the blonde take her new scarf back to the store?

It was too tight.

Why did it take the blonde a whole week to wash three basement windows?

It took her six days just to dig the holes to put the ladder in.

Did you hear about the blonde who gave her cat a bath?

She still hasn't gotten all the hair off her tongue.

How does a psychic refer to a blonde?

Light reading.

What do you call a blonde in a leather jacket?

A rebel without a clue.

Why did the blonde smell good only on her right side?

She didn't know where to buy Left Guard.

Why did the blonde put her finger over the nail she was hammering?

The noise gave her a headache.

Why do blondes have more fun?

They are so very easy to keep amused.

What does a postcard from a blonde's vacation say?

Having a wonderful time. Where am I?

Why did the blonde tiptoe past the medicine cabinet?

So she wouldn't wake up the sleeping pills.

How does a blonde hemophiliac treat herself?

Acupuncture.

Did you hear about the blonde who shot an arrow into the air?

She missed.

What's a blonde's favorite color?

A light shade of clear.

Did you hear about the blonde prisoner who was found in her cell with half a dozen bumps on her head?

She tried to hang herself with a bungee cord.

Hear about the blonde explorer?

She bought a piece of sandpaper thinking it was a map of the Sahara Desert.

Did you hear about the blonde who thought nitrates were cheaper than day rates?

A blonde lived on a farm. She didn't get many visitors, so I went to see her. When I got there, she was standing stiff as a board, out in the middle of the cow paddock. I yelled out to her and asked what she was doing standing out there all still and straight.

She replied that she was trying to win a Nobel Peace Prize.

I said, "Well, that's great, but what are you doing in the paddock?"

She replied, "I was reading the newspaper, and it said all you had to do to win the Nobel Peace Prize was to be outstanding in your field."

A blonde goes to get her hair cut. The hairstylist cuts for about thirty minutes, hands the blonde a mirror, and asks, "How do you like it?"

The blonde says, "It's okay, but could you make it just a little longer in the back?"

Why did the blonde keep ice cubes in the freezer?

To keep the refrigerator cold.

What is every blonde's ambition in life?

To be like Vanna White and learn the alphabet.

How does a blonde spell "farm"?

E-I-E-I-O.

What are the worst six years in a blonde's life?

Third grade.

What do you call a blonde CPA?

An impostor.

A blonde, wanting to earn some money, decided to hire herself out as a handyman-type and started canvassing a wealthy neighborhood. She went to the front door of the first house and asked the owner if he had any jobs for her to do.

"Well, you can paint my porch. How much will you charge?"

The blonde said, "How about fifty dollars?"

The man agreed and told her the paint and ladders that she might need were in the garage. The man's wife, inside the house, heard the conversation and said to her husband, "Does she realize that the porch goes all the way around the house?"

The man replied, "She should. She was standing on the porch."

A short time later, the blonde came to the door to collect her money.

"You're finished already?" he asked.

"Yes," the blonde answered, "and I had paint left over, so I gave it two coats."

Impressed, the man reached in his pocket for the $50.

"And by the way," the blonde added, "that's not a Porch, it's a Ferrari."

What do you call a blonde golfer with an I.Q. of 125?

A foursome.

Why did the blonde bake a chicken for three and a half days?

It said cook it for half an hour per pound, and she weighed 125.

Why can't blondes make ice cubes?

They always forget the recipe.

How do you keep a blonde in suspense?

Give her a mirror and tell her to wait for the other person to say "hi."

Why do blondes shower for hours?

The shampoo bottle says, "Lather, rinse, and repeat!"

Why does it take so long to build a blonde snowman?

You have to hollow out the head.

Why don't blondes go bald?

Because the vacuum in their head holds the hair in.

A blonde went into an appliance store looking for a TV. After a few minutes, she picked one out and approached the salesman. "I want to buy this television," she said.

The salesman replied, "Sorry, we don't serve blondes here."

She got mad and went home. She dyed her hair dark brown and returned to the store. "I want to buy this television," she said to the salesman, but she got the same response: "Sorry, miss, we don't serve blondes here."

She left again, frustrated. She went home and proceeded to shave her head, eyebrows and all, leaving no visible trace of blond hair on her head.

She returned to the store and once again approached the salesman. "Sir, I would like to purchase this television, and I don't want any problems."

To which the salesman replied, "Sorry, miss, we don't serve blondes."

Fed up, she cried, "How can you tell that I am blond? I have dyed my hair and even resorted to shaving every hair on my head!"

The salesman replied, "Well, miss, that television you are trying to buy is a microwave."

Why did the blonde have a hysterectomy?

She wanted to stop having grandchildren.

Two blondes were roofing a house. One would pull out a nail and then hammer it into the roof. Then she would pull out another nail, look at it, then throw it over her shoulder.

The second blonde eventually saw what the first blonde was doing. She watched her for a while, and finally said, "Why do you keep throwing out every other nail?"

The first blonde replied, "Because their point is on the wrong end."

The second blonde said, "You airhead, those nails are for the other side of the roof!"

BLONDE: Excuse me, sir, what time is it?

MAN: It's three-fifteen.

BLONDE: (looking puzzled) You know, it's the weirdest thing, I have been asking that question all day, and each time I get a different answer.

An airline captain was breaking in a new blonde flight attendant. The route they were flying had a layover in another city. Upon their arrival, the captain showed the flight attendant the best places for airline personnel to eat, shop, and stay overnight.

The next morning, as the pilot was preparing the crew for the day's route, he noticed the new flight attendant was missing. He knew which room she was in at the hotel and called her up wondering what happened.

She answered the phone, crying, and said she couldn't get out of her room.

"You can't get out of your room?" the captain asked, "Why not?"

The flight attendant replied, "There are only three doors in here." She sobbed, "One is the bathroom, one is the closet, and one has a sign on it that says 'Do Not Disturb'!"

Why can't blondes put in lightbulbs?

They keep breaking them with the hammers.

A blonde, brunette, and a redhead escaped from prison. They were running along when they came upon a dock. On the dock were three gunnysacks. They could hear the cops gaining on them, so the brunette suggested that they get in the sacks. So they got in the sacks right before the cops arrived.

A cop kicked the sack with the redhead in it, and she said, "Ruff ruff ruff!"

He said, "Oh, it's only a dog."

He kicked the one with the brunette in it, and she said, "Meow meow meow."

He said, "Oh, it's only a cat."

Then he kicked the one with the blonde in it, and she said, "Potatoes potatoes potatoes!"

A blonde, a brunette, and a redhead are stuck on an island. For years they live there, and one day a magic lamp washes ashore. They rub it and, sure enough, out comes a genie.

The genie says, "Since I can give out only three wishes, you may each have one."

So the brunette goes first: "I have been stuck here for years, I miss my family and my husband and my life—I just want to go home."

POOF, she is gone.

The redhead makes her wish: "This place sucks, I want to go home, too."

POOF, she is gone.

The blonde starts crying uncontrollably.

The genie asks, "What is the matter?"

The blonde says, "I wish my friends would come back."

A blonde, a brunette, and a redhead all tried out for the same job as road stripers. The boss told them they would all work for three days and whoever painted the most would get the job.

At the end of the first day, the redhead had painted 3 miles, the brunette had painted 2.5 miles, and the blonde had painted 6 miles. The boss was so excited he told her to keep it up and the job was hers.

The next day, the redhead painted 5 miles and the brunette 5.6 miles, but the blonde only painted 4 miles. The boss told her not to worry. "You still have a good lead," he said.

So on the third day, the redhead had painted 6 miles, the brunette 5 miles, and the blonde only 1 mile. The boss was so disappointed, he asked the blonde, "What went wrong? You were doing so well."

She said, "Well, that bucket of paint kept getting farther and farther away."

How do you amuse a blonde for hours?

On both sides of a piece of paper, write "please turn over."

Why did the blonde stare at the can of frozen orange juice for two hours?

Because the can said "concentrate."

How do you get a one-armed blonde out of a tree?

Wave to her.

How can you tell when a fax has been sent from a blonde?

There is a stamp on it.

Why do blondes put their hair in ponytails?

To cover up the valve stem.

What do you call a brunette with a blonde on either side?

An interpreter.

Why are there no dumb brunettes?

Peroxide.

A blonde is walking down the street with a pig under her arm. She passes a person who asks, "Where did you get that?"

The pig says, "I won her in a raffle!"

What did the blonde do when she heard that 90 percent of accidents occur around the home?

She moved.

A blonde died and went to heaven. When she got to the Pearly Gates, she met St. Peter, who said, "Before you get to come into heaven, you have to pass a test."

"Oh, no!" she said.

St. Peter said not to worry, he'd make it easy. "Who was God's son?" he asked.

The blonde thought for a few minutes and said, "Andy!"

"That's interesting. . . . What made you say that?" St. Peter asked.

She started to sing: "Andy walks with me! Andy talks with me! Andy tells me . . ."

A brunette and a blonde were walking along in a park.

The brunette said suddenly, "Awww, look at the dead birdie."

The blonde stopped, looked up, and said, "Where?"

A blonde gets on an airplane and sits down in the first-class section. The flight attendant tells her she must move to coach because she doesn't have a first-class ticket.

The blonde replies, "I'm blonde, I'm smart, I have a good job, and I'm staying in first class until we reach Jamaica."

The flight attendant gets the head flight attendant, who asks the woman to leave. She says, "I'm blonde, I'm smart, I have a good job, and I'm staying in first class until we reach Jamaica."

The flight attendants don't know what to do because the rest of the passengers need to be seated, so they get the copilot. The copilot goes up to the blonde and whispers in her ear. She immediately gets up and goes to her seat in the coach section.

The head flight attendant asks the copilot what he said to get her to move. The copilot replies, "I told her that the front half of the airplane wasn't going to Jamaica."

Here Is a Group of Medical Terms as Defined by Blondes:

Barium	What to do when treatment fails
Bowel	Letter like A E I O or U
Cauterize	Made eye contact with her
Colic	Sheepdog
Dilate	To live long
Enema	Not a friend
Fester	Quicker
Hangnail	Coat hook
Labor pain	Hurt at work
Tablet	Small table
Tumor	More than one
Varicose	Nearby
Vein	Conceited

A blonde named Anna had a near-death experience the other day when she went horseback riding. Everything was going fine until the horse started bouncing out of control. She tried with all her might to hang on, but she was thrown off. Just when things could not possibly get worse, her foot got caught in the stirrup. When this happened, she fell headfirst to the ground. Her head continued to bounce harder as the horse did not stop or even slow down. Just as she was giving up hope and losing consciousness, the department store manager happened to walk by and unplug it.

One day a blonde went up to a soda machine, put in some money, and a soda came out. She got really excited and started to put more money into the machine. The more and more she did it, the more the sodas came out.

After a while, someone walked up to her and asked her if they could please get a soda. The blonde said, "Get out of my face, I'm winning!"

Classic Blonde Jokes

What goes "Vroom-screech, vroom-screech?"

A blonde driving through a flashing red light.

What do you call an intelligent blonde?

A golden retriever.

Why do blondes write TGIF on their shoes?

Toes Go In First.

Why did the M&M manufacturer fire their blond employees?

Because they kept throwing away the W's.

A blonde got very depressed when she looked at her driver's license and saw she had an "F" in sex.

What do you call a blonde with two brain cells?

Pregnant.

How do you change a blonde's mind?

Buy her another beer.

How do you know when a blonde has been making chocolate chip cookies?

You find M&M shells all over the kitchen floor.

What's the disease that paralyzes blondes from the waist down?

Marriage.

What is a blonde's idea of safe sex?
A padded dash.

How many blondes does it take to play tag?
One.

What did the blonde get on her S.A.T.?
Nail polish.

Business

There was a man who was in a horrible accident, but the only permanent damage he suffered was the amputation of both of his ears. As a result of this unusual handicap, he became very self-conscious about having no ears.

Because of the accident, he received a large sum of money from the insurance company. It had always been his dream to own his own business, so he decided that, with all this money, he now had the means to own a business. So he went out and purchased a small, but expanding computer firm. He realized that he had no business knowledge at all, so he decided that he would have to hire someone to run the business for him.

He picked out three top candidates, and interviewed each of them. The first interview went really well. But his last question was, "Do you notice anything unusual about me?"

The guy said, "Now that you mention it, you have no ears."

The man got really upset and threw the guy out.

The second interview went even better than the first. Again, to conclude the interview, the man asked the same question: "Do you notice anything unusual about me?"

The guy also replied, "Yes, you have no ears."

The man became really upset again, and he threw the second candidate out.

Then came the third interview. The third candidate was even better than the second, the best of the lot. Almost certain that he wanted to hire this guy, the man once again asked, "Do you notice anything unusual about me?"

The guy replied, "Yeah, you're wearing contact lenses."

Surprised, the man then asked, "Wow! That's quite perceptive of you. How could you tell?"

The guy burst out laughing and said, "Well, you can't wear glasses if you don't have any ears!"

Weiss and Stein went into business together and opened a wholesale men's clothing outlet. Things went well for a year or so, but then the recession came along and they found themselves sitting on ten thousand plaid jackets, which they couldn't sell to save their souls. Just as they were discussing bankruptcy, a fellow came in and introduced himself as a buyer for a big menswear chain in Australia. "Wouldn't happen to have any plaid jackets, would you?" he asked. "They're selling like crazy down under."

Weiss looked at Stein. "Maybe we can work something out, if the price is right," he said coolly to the Aussie.

After some tough negotiating a price was agreed on, and the papers were signed. But as he was leaving, their big prospect said, "Just one thing, mates. I've got to get authorization from the home office for a deal this big. Today's Monday; if you don't get a cable from me by Friday, the deal's final."

For the next four days, Weiss and Stein paced miserably back and forth, sweating blood and wincing every time they heard footsteps outside their door. On Friday the hours crept by, but by four o'clock they figured they were home free—until there was a loud knock on the door. "Western Union!" a voice called out.

As Stein collapsed, white-faced, behind his desk, Weiss dashed to the door. A minute later, he rushed back into the office waving a telegram. "Great news, Stein," he cried jubilantly, "great news! Your mother's dead!"

One CEO always scheduled staff meetings for 4:30 on Friday afternoons. When one of the employees finally got up the nerve to ask why, the CEO explained, "I'll tell you why—it's the only time of the week when none of you seems to want to argue with me."

Performance Reviews

These quotations were allegedly taken from actual employee performance evaluations in a large American corporation.

"Since my last report, this employee has reached rock bottom . . . and has started to dig."

"His men would follow him anywhere, but only out of morbid curiosity."

"I would not allow this employee to breed."

"This employee is really not so much of a 'has-been,' but more of a definite 'won't be.'"

"Works well when under constant supervision and cornered like a rat in a trap."

"When she opens her mouth, it seems that it is only to change feet."

"He would be out of his depth in a parking lot puddle."

"This young lady has delusions of adequacy."

"He sets low personal standards and then consistently fails to achieve them."

"This employee is depriving a village somewhere of an idiot."

"This employee should go far . . . and the sooner he starts, the better."

"Got a full six-pack, but lacks the plastic thing to hold it all together."

"A gross ignoramus—144 times worse than an ordinary ignoramus."

"He certainly takes a long time to make his pointless."

"He doesn't have ulcers, but he's a carrier."

"I would like to go hunting with him sometime."

"He's been working with glue too much."

"He would argue with a signpost."

"He has a knack for making strangers immediately."

"He brings a lot of joy whenever he leaves the room."

"When his I.Q. reaches fifty, he should sell."

"If you see two people talking and one looks bored, he's the other one."

"A photographic memory, but with the lens cover glued on."

"A prime candidate for natural deselection."

"Donated his brain to science before he was done using it."

"Gates are down, the lights are flashing, but the train isn't coming."

"Has two brains: one is lost and the other is out looking for it."

"If he were any more stupid, he'd have to be watered twice a week."

"If you give him a penny for his thoughts, you'd get change."

"If you stand close enough to him, you can hear the ocean."

"It's hard to believe that he beat a million other sperm to the egg."

"One neuron short of a synapse."

"Some drink from the fountain of knowledge; he only gargled."

"Takes him two hours to watch *60 Minutes.*"

"The wheel is turning, but the hamster is dead."

Clarification of Corporate Lingo

Employer's Lingo:

"COMPETITIVE SALARY"

We remain competitive by paying less than our competitors.

"JOIN OUR FAST-PACED TEAM"

We have no time to train you.

"CASUAL WORK ATMOSPHERE"

We don't pay enough to expect that you'll dress up.

"MUST BE DEADLINE-ORIENTED"

You'll be six months behind schedule on your first day.

"DUTIES WILL VARY"

Anyone in the office can boss you around.

"MUST HAVE AN EYE FOR DETAIL"

We have no quality control.

"APPLY IN PERSON"

If you're old, fat, or ugly, you'll be told the position has been filled.

"NO PHONE CALLS PLEASE"

We've filled the job; our call for résumés is just a legal formality.

"SEEKING CANDIDATES WITH A WIDE VARIETY OF EXPERIENCE"

You'll need it to replace three people who just left.

"PROBLEM-SOLVING SKILLS A MUST"

You're walking into a company in perpetual chaos.

"REQUIRES TEAM LEADERSHIP SKILLS"

You'll have the responsibilities of a manager, without the pay or respect.

Employee's Lingo:

"I'M EXTREMELY ADEPT AT ALL MANNER OF OFFICE ORGANIZATION"

I've used Microsoft Office.

"I'M HONEST, HARDWORKING, AND DEPENDABLE"

I pilfer office supplies.

"I TAKE PRIDE IN MY WORK"

I blame others for my mistakes.

"I AM ADAPTABLE"

I've changed jobs a lot.

"I AM ON THE GO"

I'm never at my desk.

"I'M HIGHLY MOTIVATED TO SUCCEED"

The minute I find a better job, I'm outta here.

Work vs. Prison

In prison you spend the majority of your time in an 8" × 10" cell. At work you spend most of your time in a 6" × 8" cubicle.

In prison you get three meals a day. At work you only get a break for one meal, and you have to pay for that one.

In prison you get time off for good behavior. At work you get rewarded for good behavior with more work.

In prison a guard locks and unlocks all the doors for you. At work you must carry around a security card and unlock and open all the doors yourself.

In prison you can watch TV and play games. At work you get fired for watching TV and playing games.

In prison they allow your family and friends to visit. At work you cannot even speak to your family and friends.

In prison all expenses are paid by taxpayers, with no work required. At work you get to pay all the expenses to go to work and then they deduct taxes from your salary to pay for the prisoners.

In prison you spend most of your life looking through bars from the inside wanting to get out. At work you spend most of your time wanting to get out and inside bars.

Cars

A man approached the sales counter of an auto-parts store. "Excuse me," he said, "I'd like to get a new gas cap for my Yugo."

"Sure," the clerk replied. "Sounds like a fair exchange to me."

There was a young fellow who was quite inventive and was always trying out new things.

One day he thought he'd see just how fast a bicycle could go before it became uncontrollable. He asked his friend, who owned an old Mustang, if he could tie his bike to the bumper of his car to test his theory. His friend said, "Sure."

So the young man tied his bike to the back of the car

and said to his friend: "I'll ring my bike bell once if I want you to go faster, twice if I want you maintain speed, and repeatedly if I want you to slow down."

With that, off they went. Things were going pretty well, with the car driver slowly speeding up to well over sixty mph. The young fellow on the bike was handling the speed just fine. But all of a sudden a black Corvette came up beside them, and before you knew it the fellow driving the Mustang forgot all about the fellow on the bike and took to drag racing the Corvette.

A little farther down the road sat a policeman in his cruiser, radar gun at the ready. He heard the two cars before his radar flashed 105 mph.

He called into headquarters on his radio: "Hey, you guys aren't going to believe this, but there's a Corvette and a Mustang racing out here on Highway I-15, and there's a guy on a bike ringing his bell and waving his arms trying to pass them!"

A young man was so proud of his new red Cadillac that he just had to show it off, so he cruised through the bad part of town. At a stoplight, a gigantic man hauled him out of the driver's seat, drew a circle around him on the road, and told him not to step out of the circle unless he wanted to die.

The man started to demolish the Caddie, beginning with the headlights and windows, when he heard the young man laughing. He moved on to the body and engine, but in between crashes he couldn't help hearing the young man's hysterical giggles. Finally, the man came over with his crowbar and said, "What in hell you laughing at? Your fancy car's never gonna run again."

Snickering, the young man replied, "So? Ever since you've been tearing up my car, I've been stepping in and out of this circle."

Computers

You Know It's Time to Reassess Your Relationship with Your Computer When . . .

You wake up at four o'clock in the morning to go to the bathroom and you stop to check your E-mail on the way back to bed.

You turn off your computer and get an awful empty feeling, as if you just pulled the plug on a loved one.

You decide to stay in college for an additional year or two, just for the free Internet access.

You start using smileys :-) in your regular mail.

You find yourself typing "com" after every period when using a word processor.com

You can't correspond with your mother because she doesn't have a computer.

You don't know the gender of your three closest friends because they have nondescript screen names and you never bothered to ask.

You move into a new house and you decide to Netscape before you landscape.

Your family always knows where you are.

Two computer science students meet on campus one day. The first student calls out to the other, "Hey—nice bike! Where did you get it?"

"Well," replies the other, "I was walking to class the other day when this pretty young coed rides up on this bike. She jumps off, takes off all of her clothes, and says "You can have ANYTHING you want!"

"Good choice," says the first, "Her clothes probably wouldn't have fit you anyway."

Memo: To all employees
Subject: Increased productivity

Management has determined that there is no longer any need for network or software applications support. (See below.)

The goal is to remove all computers from the desktop by December 31, 1999. Instead, everyone will be provided with an Etch A Sketch. There are many sound reasons for doing this:

1. No Y2K problems.

2. No technical glitches keeping work from being done.

3. No more wasted time reading and writing E-mails.

Frequently Asked Questions for Etch A Sketch *Technical Support:*

Q: My Etch A Sketch has all of these funny little lines all over the screen.
A: Pick it up and shake it.

Q: How do I turn my Etch A Sketch off?
A: Pick it up and shake it.

Q: What's the shortcut for Undo?
A: Pick it up and shake it.

Q: How do I create a New Document window?
A: Pick it up and shake it.

Q: How do I set the background and foreground to the same color?
A: Pick it up and shake it.

Q: What is the proper procedure for rebooting my Etch A Sketch?
A: Pick it up and shake it.

Q: How do I delete a document on my Etch A Sketch?
A: Pick up and shake it.

Q: How do I save my Etch A Sketch document?
A: Don't shake it.

The Computer-Illiterate Support Call

"Hello, Raymond Michaels, computer assistant, may I help you?"

"Yes, well, I'm having trouble with WordPerfect."

"What sort of trouble?"

"Well, I was just typing along, and all of a sudden the words went away."

"Went away?"

"They disappeared."

"Hmm. So what does your screen look like now?"

"Nothing."

"Nothing?"

"It's blank. It won't accept anything when I type."

"Are you still in WordPerfect or did you get out?"

"How do I tell?"

[Uh-oh. Well, let's give it a try anyway.) "Can you see the C-prompt on the screen?"

"What's a sea prompt?"

[Uh-huh. I thought so. Let's try a different tactic.) "Never mind. Can you move the cursor around on the screen?"

"There isn't any cursor: I told you, it won't accept anything I type."

[Ah, at least he knows what a cursor is. Sounds like a hardware problem. I wonder if he kicked out his monitor's power plug.] "Does your monitor have a power indicator?"

"What's a monitor?"

"It's the thing with the screen on it that looks like a TV. Does it have a little light that tells you when it's on?"

"I don't know."

"Well, then look at the back of the monitor and find where the power cord goes into it. Can you see that?"

[Sound of rustling and jostling] "Yes, I think so."

"Great! Follow the cord to the plug and tell me if it's plugged into the wall."

[*Pause*] "Yes, it is."

[Hmm. Well, that's interesting. I doubt he would have accidentally turned it off, and I don't want to send him hunting for the power switch because I don't know what kind of monitor he has and it's bound to have more than one switch on it. Maybe the video cable is loose or something.] "When you were behind the monitor, did you notice that there were two cables plugged into the back of it, not just one?"

"No."

"Well, there are. I need you to look back there again and find the other cable."

"Okay, here it is."

"Follow it for me and tell me if it's plugged securely into the back of your computer."

"I can't reach it."

"Uh-huh. Well, can you *see* if it is?"

"No."

"Even if you maybe put your knee on something and lean way over?"

"Oh, it's not because I don't have the right angle—it's because it's dark."

"Dark?"

"Yes. The office light is off and the only light I have is coming from the window."

"Well, turn on the office light then."

"I can't."

"No? Why not?"

"Because there's a power outage."

"A power—" *[AAAAAAAArgh!]* "A power outage? Aha! Okay, we've got it licked now. Do you still have the boxes and manuals and packing stuff your computer came in?"

"Well, yes, I kept them in the closet."

"Good! Go get them, unplug your system, and pack it up just like it was when you got it. Then take it back to the store you bought it from."

"Really? Is it that bad?"

"Yes, I'm afraid it is."

"Well, all right then, I suppose. What do I tell them?"

"Tell them you're *too stupid to own a computer.*"

[Click]

How to Tell if You Are a Geek

If ten of the following characteristics apply to you, the penny loafer with the penny inside fits.

You can quote scenes from any Monty Python movie.

Dilbert is your hero, and you display Dilbert comics throughout your work area.

You can name six *Star Trek* episodes.

Your spouse sends you an E-mail to call you to dinner.

You look forward to Christmas only to put together the kids' toys.

You have used coat hangers and duct tape for something other than hanging coats and taping ducts.

You window-shop at electronics stores.

Your ideal evening consists of fast-forwarding through

the latest science-fiction movie looking for technical inaccuracies.

You don't even know where the cover to your personal computer is.

You know the direction the water swirls when you flush.

You once took the back off your TV just to see what's inside.

You burned down the gymnasium with your Science Fair project.

You are currently gathering the components to build your own nuclear reactor.

You own one or more white short-sleeve dress shirts.

You have never backed up your hard drive.

You are aware that computers are actually good only for playing games, but you are afraid to say it out loud.

You truly believe aliens are living among us.

You tend to save the power cords from broken appliances.

You still own a slide rule, and you know how to work it.

You own a set of itty-bitty screwdrivers, but you don't remember where they are.

You rotate your screen savers more frequently than your automobile tires.

You have a functioning home copier machine, but every toaster you own turns bread into charcoal.

You have more toys than your kids.

You need a checklist to turn on the TV.

You have on occasion introduced your kids by the wrong name.

You have a habit of destroying things in order to see how they work.

Your I.Q. is a higher number than your weight.

Your father sat two inches in front of your family's first color TV with a magnifying lens to see how they made the colors, and you grew up thinking that was normal.

You can type seventy words a minute but can't read your own handwriting.

People groan at the party when you pick out the music.

You can't remember where you parked your car for the third time this week.

You ran the sound system for your senior prom.

Your checkbook always balances.

Your wristwatch has more buttons than a telephone.

You have more friends on the Internet than in real life.

You thought the real heroes of *Apollo 13* were the mission controllers.

You think that when people around you yawn, it's because they didn't get enough sleep.

You spend more on your home computer than on your car.

You know what "http" stands for.

You've tried to repair a $5 radio.

You have a neatly sorted collection of old bolts and nuts in your garage.

Your three-year-old son asks why the sky is blue, and you try to explain atmospheric absorption theory.

Your laptop computer costs more than your car.

Your four basic food groups are caffeine, fat, sugar, and chocolate.

You spend half of a plane trip with your laptop on your lap . . . and your child in the overhead compartment.

You try to hum to communicate with a modem. You succeed.

Doctors

"Yeah, Doc, what's the news?" answered Fred when his doctor called with his test results.

"I have some bad news and some really bad news," admitted the doctor. "The bad news is that you only have twenty-four hours to live."

"Oh my God," gasped Fred, sinking to his knees. "What could be worse news than that?"

"I couldn't get ahold of you yesterday."

PATIENT: I'm in a hospital!? Why am I in here?

DOCTOR: You've had an accident involving a train.

PATIENT: What happened?

DOCTOR: Well, I've got some good news and some bad news. Which would you like to hear first?

PATIENT: Well . . . the bad news first.

DOCTOR: Your legs were injured so badly that we had to amputate both of them.

PATIENT: That's terrible! What's the good news?

DOCTOR: There's a guy in the next ward who made a very good offer on your shoes.

Upon completing his examination of his patient, a doctor told him to get dressed. "I'm afraid your condition is fairly poor." The doctor sighed. "The best thing for you to do would be to give up liquor, stop smoking, give up all that rich food you've been eating at fancy restaurants, and stop seeing all those young women who keep you out until all hours."

The patient thought for a moment. "What's the next best thing?"

A woman wailed to her psychiatrist, "Oh, Doctor, what am I going to do? My husband thinks he's a refrigerator."

"Why exactly does that bother you?" the perplexed doctor asked.

"When he sleeps with his mouth open, the light keeps me up!"

"Doctor," the patient demanded, "you have a lot of nerve charging me three hundred fifty dollars just to paint my throat."

"What did you want for three hundred fifty dollars? Wallpaper?"

A psychiatrist was administering a Rorschach inkblot test to his patient. The doctor showed the first blot and asked what it resembled.

"That's two poodles having sex," replied the patient.

The second ink blot: "That's a naked lady leaning out a window, telling all the men who go by to come in and have sex with her."

The doctor showed the third inkblot. "That's a pair of crotchless underpants," the patient said.

Just then the hour was up. The doctor said, "I'm afraid that's all we have time for today."

The patient stood up and put on his hat, but before he left, he leaned over and whispered to the doctor, "Say, Doc, have you got any more of those dirty pictures?"

An artist asked the gallery owner if there had been any interest in his paintings that were on display.

"I have good news and bad news," the owner replied. "The good news is that a gentleman inquired about your work and wondered if it would appreciate in value after your death. When I told him it would, he bought all fifteen of your paintings."

"That's wonderful," the artist exclaimed. "What's the bad news?"

"The gentleman was your doctor."

One day, an older fellow was in a clinic for a checkup. After his examination, his doctor was amazed.

"Holy cow! Mr. Edwards, I must say that you are in the greatest shape of any sixty-four-year-old I have ever examined!"

"Did I say I was sixty-four?"

"Well, no, did I read your chart wrong?"

"Damn straight you did! I'm eighty-five!"

"Eighty-five! Unbelievable! You would be in great shape if you were twenty-five! How old was your father when he died?"

"Did I say he was dead?"

"You mean—"

"Damn straight! He's a hundred and six and going strong!"

"My lord! What a healthy family you must come from! How long did your grandfather live?"

"Did I say he was dead?"

"No! You can't mean—"

"Damn straight! He's a hundred twenty-six, and getting married next week!"

"A hundred twenty-six! Truly amazing, Mr. Edwards. But, gee, I wouldn't think a man would want to get married at that age!"

"Did I say he *wanted* to get married . . . ?"

A man being treated by a female psychiatrist said one day, "I keep dreaming that you're my mother."

The psychiatrist replied, "Don't worry about it, that's transference. It happens all the time."

As the man was leaving, the psychiatrist said, "Where are your overshoes?"

He replied, "I don't have any."

The psychiatrist replied, "What's wrong with you? Do you want to catch your death of cold?"

A young woman peered up from her hospital bed at the extremely handsome doctor who was examining her chart. She fluttered her eyelids and said, "They tell me that you're a real lady killer."

The doctor smiled and shook his head. "No, I make no distinction between the sexes."

A sign in a hospital emergency ward:

Interns think of God.

Residents pray to God.

Doctors believe they're God.

Nurses are God.

"Brace yourself, Mr. Collins," the physician told the patient on whom he had performed a battery of costly tests. "You have approximately six months to live."

"But I don't have insurance, Doctor," said Collins, "and I can't skimp and save enough to pay you in that time!"

"All right, all right," soothed the doctor. "Let's say nine months, then."

A man went to his dentist because he felt something wrong in his mouth. The dentist examined him and said, "That new upper plate that I put in six months ago is eroding. What have you been eating?"

The man replied, "All I can think of is that about four months ago, my wife made some asparagus and put some stuff on it that was delicious . . . hollandaise sauce. I loved it so much I now put it on everything . . . meat, toast, fish, vegetables, everything."

"Well," said the dentist. "That's probably the problem. Hollandaise sauce is made with lots of lemon juice, which is highly corrosive. It's eating away at your upper plate. I'll make you a new plate, and this time I'll use chrome."

"Why chrome?" asked the patient.

The dentist replied, "It's simple. Everyone knows that there's no plate like chrome for the hollandaise!"

A man went to his doctor to find out the results of a series of tests he'd been given the previous week. Unfortunately, his worst fears were confirmed.

"I'm afraid I have some rather bad news for you," his doctor began. "You're going to die in four weeks."

Naturally, the man was distraught. "Doctor, that's terrible! But I want a second opinion."

"Okay, you're also ugly."

A bishop was sitting in a doctor's waiting room when a red-faced and sobbing nun rushed out of the doctor's office. The bishop charged into the office and demanded to know what the doctor had done.

"I told her she was pregnant," the doctor replied.

"It couldn't be true," said the outraged bishop. "Why ever would you tell her something like that?"

"Well, it sure cured her hiccups."

The following quotes were taken from actual medical records as dictated by physicians.

By the time he was admitted, his rapid heart had stopped, and he was feeling better.

Patient has chest pain if she lies on her left side for over a year.

On the second day the knee was better and on the third day it had completely disappeared.

The patient has been depressed ever since she began seeing me in 1983.

The patient is tearful and crying constantly. She also appears to be depressed.

Discharge status: Alive but without permission.

Healthy-appearing decrepit sixty-nine-year-old male, mentally alert but forgetful.

The patient refused an autopsy.

The patient has no past history of suicides.

The patient expired on the floor uneventfully.

Patient has left his white blood cells at another hospital.

The patient's past medical history has been remarkably insignificant, with only a forty-pound weight gain in the past three days.

She slipped on the ice and apparently her legs went in separate directions in early December.

The patient experienced sudden onset of severe shortness of breath with a picture of acute pulmonary edema at home while having sex which gradually deteriorated in the emergency room.

The patient had waffles for breakfast and anorexia for lunch.

Between you and me, we ought to be able to get this lady pregnant.

The patient was in his usual state of good health until his airplane ran out of gas and crashed.

She is numb from her toes down.

The skin was moist and dry.

Occasional, constant, infrequent headaches.

Coming from Detroit, this man has no children.

Patient was alert and unresponsive.

When she fainted, her eyes rolled around the room.

Ever since he graduated from high school, Brian spent most of his waking hours lounging on the couch, watching sports programs, and drinking beer. One day, as he reached for another can, he tumbled off the sofa onto his head and had to be rushed to the hospital. After X rays were taken, the doctor went right to Brian's bedside.

"I'm sorry, but I have some bad news for you, young man. Your X rays show that you've broken a vertebra in your neck. I'm afraid you'll never work again."

"Thanks, Doc. Now what's the bad news?"

Sam and John were out cutting wood, and John cut off his arm. Sam wrapped the arm in a plastic bag and took it and John to a surgeon.

The surgeon said, "You're in luck! I'm an expert at reattaching limbs! Come back in four hours." So Sam left and when he returned in four hours, the surgeon said, "I got done faster than I expected. John is down at the local pub."

Sam went to the pub, and there was John throwing darts.

A few weeks later, Sam and John were cutting wood again, and John cut his leg off. Sam put the leg in a plastic bag and took it and John back to the surgeon.

The surgeon said, "Legs are a little tougher. Come back in six hours."

Sam left and when he returned in six hours, the surgeon said, "I finished early. John's down at the soccer field."

Sam went to the soccer field, and there was John kicking goals.

A few weeks later, John had a terrible accident and cut his head off. Sam put the head in a plastic bag and took it and the rest of John to the surgeon.

The surgeon said, "Gee, heads are really tough. Come back in twelve hours."

So Sam left and when he returned in twelve hours the surgeon said, "I'm sorry, John died."

Sam said, "I understand—heads are tough."

The surgeon said, "Oh, no! The surgery went fine! John suffocated in that plastic bag."

After his annual physical examination, an elderly patient asked his doctor, "Tell me, how long am I going to live?"

"Don't worry," his doctor replied. "You'll probably live to be eighty."

"But Doctor, I *am* eighty," he said.

"See? What did I tell you?"

Kids

Children were called upon in a classroom to make sentences with words chosen by the teacher. The teacher smiled when Jack, a slow learner, raised his hand to participate during the challenge of making a sentence with the words "Defeat," "Defense," "Deduct," and "Detail."

Jack stood thinking for a while, all eyes focused on him while his classmates awaited his reply. Smiling, he then proudly shouted out, "Defeat of deduct went over defense before detail."

Two six-year-old boys were attending religious school and giving the teachers problems. The teachers had tried everything to make them behave—time-outs, notes home, missed recesses—but could do nothing with them.

Finally the boys were sent to see the priest.

The first boy went in and sat in a chair across the desk from the priest. The priest asked, "Son, do you know where God is?"

The little boy just sat there.

The priest stood up and asked, "Son, do you know where God is?"

The little boy trembled but said nothing.

The priest leaned across the desk and again asked, "Do you know where God is?"

The little boy bolted out of the chair, rushed past his friend in the waiting room, and ran all the way home. He got in bed and pulled the covers up over his head.

His friend followed him home. He came into the bedroom and asked, "What happened in there?"

The boy replied, "God is missing, and they think we did it!"

BOY: Isn't the principal a dummy!?

GIRL: Say, do you know who I am?

BOY: No.

GIRL: I'm the principal's daughter.

BOY: And do you know who I am?

GIRL: No.

BOY: Thank goodness!

TEACHER: How old were you on your last birthday?

STUDENT: Seven.

TEACHER: How old will you be on your next birthday?

STUDENT: Nine.

TEACHER: That's impossible.

STUDENT: No, it isn't. I'm eight today.

TEACHER: If you had one dollar and you asked your father for another, how many dollars would you have?

VINCENT: One dollar.

TEACHER (sadly): You don't know your arithmetic.

VINCENT (sadly): You don't know my father.

TEACHER: George, go to the map and find North America.

GEORGE: Here it is!

TEACHER: Correct. Now, class, who discovered America?

CLASS: George!

TEACHER: Billy, name one important thing we have today that we didn't have ten years ago.

BILLY: Me!

SUBSTITUTE TEACHER: Are you chewing gum?

BILLY: No, I'm Billy Anderson.

TEACHER: Sammy, how can one person make so many stupid mistakes in one day?

SAMMY: I get up early.

TOMMY: Teacher, would you punish me for something I didn't do?

TEACHER: Of course not.

TOMMY: Good, because I didn't do my homework.

TEACHER: I hope I didn't see you looking at Don's paper.

GARY: I hope you didn't either.

JOHN: I don't think I deserve a zero on this test.

TEACHER: I agree, but it's the lowest mark I can give you.

TEACHER: Well, at least there's one thing I can say about your son.

FATHER: What's that?

TEACHER: With grades like these, he couldn't be cheating.

TEACHER: Ellen, give me a sentence starting with "I."

ELLEN: I is—

TEACHER: No, Ellen. Always say, "I am."

ELLEN: All right . . . "I am the ninth letter of the alphabet."

A three-year-old went with his dad to see a litter of kittens. On returning home, he breathlessly informed his mother there were two boy kittens and two girl kittens.

"How did you know?" his mother asked.

"Daddy picked them up and looked underneath," he replied. "I think it's printed on the bottom."

A farmer was helping one of his cows give birth when he noticed his four-year-old son standing at the fence with wide eyes, taking in the whole event. The man thought to himself, Great! He's four years old, and I'm gonna have to start explaining the birds and bees now. No need to jump the gun—I guess I'll let him ask and then I'll answer.

After everything was over, the man walked over to his son and said, "Well, son, do you have any questions?"

"Just one," gasped the still-wide-eyed lad. "How fast was that calf going when he hit that cow?"

The little girl had just listened to her mother reading one of her favorite fairy tales.

"Mommy," asked the child, "do all fairy tales begin with 'Once upon a time . . .'?"

"No, dearest," replied the mother. "Sometimes they start with, 'Darling, I have to work a little late at the office tonight. . . .' "

Here's Some Advice from Kids, Aged Eight to Fourteen:

Never trust a dog to watch your food.

When you want something expensive, ask your grandparents.

Never smart off to a teacher whose eyes and ears are twitching.

Wear a hat when feeding seagulls.

Sleep in your clothes so you'll be dressed in the morning.

Never ask for anything that costs more than five dollars when your parents are doing taxes.

Never bug a pregnant mom.

Don't ever be too full for dessert.

When your dad is mad and asks you, "Do I look stupid?" don't answer him.

Never tell your mom her diet's not working.

Don't pick on your sister when she's holding a baseball bat.

When you get a bad grade in school, show it to your mom when she's on the phone.

Never try to baptize a cat.

Never spit when on a roller coaster.

Never do pranks at a police station.

Beware of cafeteria food when it looks like it's moving.

Never tell your little brother that you're not going to do what your mom told you to do.

Never dare your little brother to paint the family car.

Forget the cake. Go for the icing!

A father took his three-year-old son grocery shopping, and the boy was sitting in the special shopping-cart seat provided for children. Thus, he had a very good view of everything and was quite busy taking it all in.

When they got to the checkout line, they were in back of an enormously broad lady whose shopping cart was full to the point of collapsing. After a couple of minutes, the father began to get very nervous because he saw how entranced and wide-eyed his son was with the huge lady and her overflowing shopping cart, and he knew it would be only a matter of time before his son would say something, possibly something impolite. Yet, he dared not try to distract his son because he thought that breaking the boy's trance would cause the boy to say whatever he was thinking . . . and sooner rather than later.

Just then the beeper the lady was wearing on the back of her belt began beeping. The little boy looked up at his father and said, "Look out, Dad. She's backing up!"

A first-grade teacher collected old, well-known proverbs. She gave each kid in her class the first half of a proverb and had them come up with the rest. Here are the results:

As You Shall Make Your Bed, So Shall You . . . Mess It Up.

Better Be Safe Than . . . Punch a Fifth Grader.

Strike While the . . . Bug Is Close.

It's Always Darkest Before . . . Daylight Savings Time.

Never Underestimate the Power of . . . Termites.

You Can Lead a Horse to Water But . . . How?

Don't Bite the Hand That . . . Looks Dirty.

No News Is . . . Impossible.

A Miss Is as Good as a . . . Mr.

You Can't Teach an Old Dog New . . . Math.

If You Lie Down with the Dogs, You'll . . . Stink in the Morning.

The Pen Is Mightier Than the . . . Pigs.

An Idle Mind Is . . . the Best Way to Relax.

Where There's Smoke, There's . . . Pollution.

Happy the Bride Who . . . Gets All the Presents!

A Penny Saved Is . . . Not Much.

Two's Company, Three's . . . the Musketeers.

Don't Put off Tomorrow What . . . You Put on to Go to Bed.

Laugh and the Whole World Laughs with You, Cry and . . . You Have to Blow Your Nose.

Children Should Be Seen and Not . . . Spanked or Grounded.

If at First You Don't Succeed . . . Get New Batteries.

You Get out of Something What You . . . See Pictured on the Box.

When the Blind Leadeth the Blind . . . Get out of the Way.

One day, a toddler put her shoes on by herself. Her mother noticed the right shoe was on the left foot. She said, "Honey, your shoes are on the wrong feet."

The little girl looked up at her with a raised brow and said, "Don't kid me, Mom. I *know* they're my feet."

On the first day of school, the kindergarten teacher said, "If anyone has to go to the bathroom, hold up two fingers."

A little voice from the back of the room asked, "How will that help?"

One night while saying his prayers, a little boy was heard to finish, "God bless Mommy, God bless Daddy, God bless Grandma, good-bye Grandpa." The next day his grandfather dropped dead of a heart attack.

A few weeks later, the little boy was praying, "God bless Mommy, God bless Daddy, good-bye Grandma." The next day his poor grandmother was hit by a bus while crossing the street—she never felt a thing.

A month or so later, the little boy was praying and said, "God bless Mommy, good-bye Daddy." His father panicked. He spent the next day using extreme caution in everything he did at work, and it took him forty-five minutes to make the usual ten-minute drive home in the evening. He was met at the front door by his wife, who said, "What do you think happened today, dear? The most awful thing—the milkman dropped dead on the back porch."

A mother and her young son returned from the grocery store and began putting away the groceries. The boy opened the box of animal crackers and spread them all over the table.

"What are you doing?" his mother asked.

"The box says you can't eat them if the seal is broken," the boy explained. "I'm looking for the seal."

Little Johnny was doing very badly in math. His parents had tried everything—tutors, flash cards, special learning centers—in short, everything that they could think of.

Finally in a last-ditch effort, they took Johnny down and enrolled him in the local Catholic school.

After the first day, little Johnny came home with a very serious look on his face. He didn't kiss his mother hello. Instead, he went straight to his room and started studying. Books and paper were spread out all over the room, and Johnny was hard at work. His mother was amazed.

Later, she called him down to dinner, and, to her shock, the minute he was done he marched right back to his room without a word. In no time he was back hitting the books as hard as before.

This went on for some time, day after day, while his mother tried to understand what had brought about such a profound difference.

Finally, little Johnny brought home his report card. He quietly laid it on the table, went up to his room, and hit the books. With great trepidation, his mother looked at the report card. To her surprise, Johnny got an A in math.

She could no longer hold her curiosity. She went to his room and said, "Son, what was it? Was it the nuns?"

Little Johnny looked at her and shook his head no.

"Well then," she asked, "was it the books? Are they better? Was it the discipline, the structure, the uniforms—*what was it?*"

Little Johnny looked at her and said, "Well, on the first day of school, when I saw that guy nailed to the plus sign, I knew they weren't fooling around."

A father often read Bible stories to his young children. One day he read, "The man named Lot was warned to take his wife and flee out of the city, but his wife looked back and was turned to salt."

His son asked, "What happened to the flea?"

A sweet little boy surprised his grandmother one morning and brought her a cup of coffee in bed. He had made it all by himself and was so proud. He waited eagerly to hear her verdict on the quality of the coffee.

The grandmother had truly never in her life had such a bad cup of coffee. The first few sips just about did her in, but she praised her grandson, told him it was wonderful, and drank it all anyway.

As she forced down the last sip, she noticed three little green army guys in the bottom of the cup. She asked, "Honey, why would three of your little army guys be in the bottom of my cup?"

Her grandson replied, "You know, Grandma, it's like on TV: 'The best part of waking up is soldiers in your cup.' "

Kids on Science

These notions about science were culled from essays, exams, and classroom discussions. Most came from fifth and sixth graders.

A vibration is a motion that cannot make up its mind which way it wants to go.

Genetics explains why you look like your father and if you don't why you should.

Vacuums are nothings. We only mention them to let them know we know they're there.

Some oxygen molecules help fires burn while others help make water, so sometimes it's brother against brother.

We say the cause of perfume disappearing is evaporation.

To most people solutions mean finding the answers. But to chemists solutions are things that are all mixed up.

In looking at a drop of water under a microscope, we find there are twice as many H's as O's.

Clouds just keep circling the Earth around and around. There is not much else to do.

Water vapor gets together in a cloud. When it is big enough to be called a drop, it does.

Humidity is the experience of looking for air and finding water.

We keep track of the humidity in the air so we won't drown when we breathe.

Rain is saved up in cloud banks.

One horsepower is the amount of energy it takes to drag a horse 500 feet in one second.

You can listen to thunder after lightning and tell how close you came to getting hit. If you don't hear it, you got hit, so never mind.

Talc is found on rocks and babies.

The law of gravity says no fair jumping up without coming back down.

When they broke open molecules, they found they were only stuffed with atoms. But when they broke open atoms, they found them stuffed with explosions.

When people run around and around in circles, we say they are crazy. When planets do it, we say they are orbiting.

Rainbows are just to look at, not to really understand.

While the Earth seems to be knowingly keeping its distance from the sun, it is really only centrificating.

Someday we may discover how to make magnets that can point in any direction.

South America has cold summers and hot winters, but somehow they still manage.

Most books now say our sun is a star. But it knows how to change back into a sun in the daytime.

Water freezes at 32 degrees and boils at 212 degrees. There are 180 degrees between freezing and boiling because there are 180 degrees between north and south.

There are twenty-six vitamins in all, but some of the letters are yet to be discovered. Finding them all means living forever.

There is a tremendous weight pushing down on the center of the Earth because of so much population stomping around up there these days.

Lime is a green-tasting rock.

Many dead animals in the past changed to fossils while others preferred to be oil.

Some people can tell what time it is by looking at the sun. But I have never been able to make out the numbers.

In some rocks you can find the fossil footprints of fishes.

Cyanide is so poisonous that one drop of it on a dog's tongue will kill the strongest man.

A blizzard is when it snows sideways.

A hurricane is a breeze of a big size.

A monsoon is a French gentleman.

Thunder is a rich source of loudness.

Isotherms and isobars are even more important than their names sound.

It is so hot in some places that the people there have to live in other places.

The wind is like the air, only pushier.

Lawyers

A man was standing in line waiting to go into a movie theater when he suddenly felt the guy behind him massaging his shoulders. He turned around and said, "Hey, what the hell are you doing?"

The guy stammered, "Oh, I'm terribly sorry. It's just that I'm a chiropractor, and I could tell you were pretty tense, and without even realizing it, I started to rub your shoulders to release the tension and help you relax."

"That's hogwash," the man cried. "I'm a lawyer, and you don't see me screwing the guy in front of me!"

A truck driver was tooling down the highway when he saw a priest at the side of the road. Naturally, he stopped to pick up the priest.

Farther down the road the truck driver noticed a lawyer on the side of the road. He aimed his truck directly at the lawyer. Then he thought, Oh, no, I have a priest in the truck, I can't run down this lawyer. So, at the last second, the truck driver swerved to miss the lawyer.

But the truck driver heard a thump outside of the truck. He looked in his rearview mirror but didn't see anything. He turned to the priest and said, "Sorry, Father, I just missed that lawyer at the side of the road."

And the priest said, "Don't worry, son, I got him with my door."

An attorney had just finished a consultation with an elderly, nearly blind widow, for which he charged her $100. The widow opened her purse and removed a $100 bill. When the lawyer accepted it, he noticed there was another $100 bill stuck to it. Immediately the lawyer's keen legal mind realized he was faced with a vital ethical question:

Should he tell his partner?

A busy, slightly obsessive young lawyer decided that he badly needed a hobby. Since his buddies talked about sailing all the time, he decided he'd give it a go. He went to the local boat show and asked a lot of questions. Everything seemed to be going well. Then the lawyer asked, "How do you dock the boat?"

The salesman replied, "Well, you really don't dock the sailboat, you tie it up to a float just beyond the dock. This way you don't bang up the finish on the craft."

"Well then," the lawyer asked, "how do you get out to the sailboat?"

"Good question." The salesman told him that you can get a small raft and paddle out to the boat, or just walk out to the boat, if you don't mind getting wet.

"Oh, I get it," the lawyer replied. "It's Row vs. Wade."

A woman and her little girl were visiting the grave of the little girl's grandmother. On their way through the cemetery back to the car, the little girl asked, "Mommy, do they ever bury two people in the same grave?"

"Of course not, dear," replied the mother. "Why would you think that?"

"The tombstone back there said, 'Here lies a lawyer and an honest man.' "

A man walked into a curio store and began browsing.

After a while, he brought a brass rat up to the counter. The proprietor said, "That will be ten dollars for the brass rat and a thousand dollars for the story behind it."

The man said, "Thanks, but I'll just pay the ten dollars and pass on the story."

He purchased the brass rat and left the store. As he was walking down the street, he started to notice all sorts of rats following him—hundreds of them. The farther he walked, the more rats followed. He walked down to a wharf and still more rats came out to follow him. He decided to walk out into the water, and all the rats followed him and drowned.

He returned to the store immediately. The proprietor said, "Aha! You came back to pay the thousand dollars for the story, right?"

"No," replied the man. "I came back to see if you have any brass lawyers."

A lawyer opened the door of his BMW when suddenly a car came along and hit the door, ripping it off completely. When the police arrived at the scene, the lawyer was complaining bitterly about the damage to his precious BMW.

"Officer, look what they've done to my beautiful BMW!" he whined.

"You lawyers are so materialistic, you make me sick!" retorted the officer. "You're so worried about your stupid car that you didn't even notice that your left arm was ripped off!"

"Oh, my God!" replied the lawyer, finally noticing the bloody left shoulder where his arm once was. "Where's my Rolex?!"

A fairly successful businessman in his early thirties was getting lonely for some companionship. He was fairly well off, lived in a nice apartment, had refined tastes, but somehow or other he could never find the perfect companion. Finally, he had an inspiration.

He strolled into a pet shop and explained his problem

to the sympathetic clerk. The clerk thought for a moment, then said, "I have the perfect pet for you, sir," He disappeared into the back of the shop and emerged with a small cardboard box.

The businessman opened the box and discovered a frog. "A frog?" he asked disbelievingly.

"Ah," said the salesman, "but not just any frog. I really think you'll be surprised with this pet. May I suggest you take it home for a trial. If it does not meet with your satisfaction, feel free to bring it back within a week for a full refund."

What did he have to lose? He paid the clerk, put the box under his arm, and headed home. When he arrived, he set the box in a corner, took the lid off so the frog could breathe, and looked at it for a moment. Nothing special.

He went across the room to his bar and mixed himself a martini, but just as he brought the glass to his lips, he was startled to hear a voice say, "Excuse me."

He looked around. There was no one there. He locked the door. Since he lived on the seventh floor, there couldn't possibly be anyone outside the window. Confused, he pondered for a moment, then shrugged and raised the glass again.

And again, loud and clear: "Pardon me."

The man glanced at the box. The voice seemed to be coming from the frog.

"Yes, over here."

Perplexed, he leaned over the box. The frog looked up at him.

I couldn't help noticing that you made yourself an excellent martini, there."

The man was astonished. "You . . . you *talk?*"

The frog chuckled. "Oh, of course I talk. But that martini . . . Well, I just happen to be a very particular martini drinker, and you mixed that one exactly the way I like mine, not too dry, not too—"

The man recovered his poise. "Would you care for one?"

The frog hopped gratefully out of its box. "Why, thank you. Most people are uncomfortable around frogs, I know, but I can see this is going to be different."

The two got to talking, and they really hit it off right away. The frog had the same taste in classical music as the man did, they both appreciated impressionist paintings, and both of them liked to watch weekend tennis matches.

When it came time for dinner, the man carried the frog into the kitchen. The frog offered suggestions on how to marinate the hanger steak, selected the perfect wine to accompany, and kept up a steady flow of witty conversation throughout the evening. The man was delighted. The frog was, indeed, everything the pet-store clerk had promised.

Presently, the man began to feel tired, so he set the frog gently in its box and brought it into the bedroom. As he prepared to turn out the lights, the frog discreetly cleared its throat.

"I wonder . . ." the frog began tentatively, "I wonder if you would mind very much—"

"What is it?" the man asked.

"Well," the frog said, "I feel so close to you . . . I mean, we share so many interests, we've eaten and drunk together . . . I just somehow wouldn't feel right sleeping in a box. Do you think I might possibly just sleep on the pillow next to you?"

Well, the man saw nothing wrong with this request, so he lifted the frog out of its box and set it on the pillow. He bade it good night, turned out the lights, and got into bed.

He was just dozing off when he heard another discreet cough.

"Excuse me," the frog whispered. "I really hate to ask this, and don't think I mean anything by it, but . . ." The frog paused.

The man sighed. "What do you want?"

The frog shifted about uncomfortably. "Well, it's just that I've grown accustomed to . . . that is, you see, I've always been kissed good night before."

The man shook his head. "No. I'm sorry, but no matter how unique you are, you're still a frog."

The frog interrupted. "No, no, nothing like that. Just a quick little peck on the forehead. Really. It would mean so much to me. . . ."

Well, the frog sounded so plaintive, and it really was such a wonderful addition to his life, that he decided that a kiss couldn't possibly do any harm. He leaned over and kissed the frog.

There was a puff of blue smoke, and when it cleared, the man found himself in bed next to a stunningly beautiful blond teenage girl, smiling blissfully up at him.

"And that, your Honor, is how my client came to be . . ."

A dog ran into a butcher's shop, grabbed a string of sausages, and ran back out again. The irate butcher recognized the dog as belonging to one of his regular customers, a lawyer, so that afternoon he went to the lawyer's office and said to the lawyer, "If a dog steals meat from my store, do I have the right to demand payment from the dog's owner?"

The lawyer replied, "Yes, absolutely."

"Well," said the butcher, "you owe me nine dollars for the sausages your dog stole this morning."

The lawyer sighed and wrote out a check for $9.

A week later the butcher received an envelope from the lawyer containing a bill for $50 for consultation.

What do you call a hundred lawyers skydiving out of an airplane?

Skeet.

A defending attorney was cross-examining a coroner. The attorney asked, "Before you signed the death certificate, had you taken the man's pulse?"

The coroner said, "No."

The attorney then asked, "Did you listen for a heartbeat?"

"No."

"Did you check for breathing?"

"No."

"So when you signed the death certificate, you had not taken any steps to make sure the man was dead, had you?"

The coroner, weary of the browbeating, said, "Well, let me put it this way. The man's brain was sitting in a jar on my desk, but for all I know he could be out there practicing law somewhere."

A rabbit and a snake, both blind from birth, happened to meet in the forest one day. They got to talking, and the rabbit, not knowing what a snake looked like, asked the snake, "Would you mind running your hands over my body and telling me what kind of an animal I am? I'm too embarrassed to ask my sighted friends. I'm afraid they'll make fun of me."

The snake said, "Okay," and proceeded to wind himself around the rabbit from one end to the other, then back again. "Well," the snake said at last, "You're kind of warm, with real soft fur, and you have two very long, furry ears."

The rabbit thought about that for a moment and then exclaimed, "Wow! I must be a bunny rabbit!" and he hopped happily around in a circle and then began hopping away.

"Wait!" called the snake. "What about me? Come back and do the same thing for me!"

The rabbit hopped over and with his furry paws, he patted the snake from one end to the other and then back again.

"Well?" asked the snake. "What kind of animal am I?"

"I'm not really sure," said the rabbit. "You're kind of

cold and slimy, and for the life of me, I can't tell your head from your butt."

The snake thought and thought about this, then exclaimed, "Wow! I must be an attorney!"

A man and his wife decided it was time to find out what their son wanted to be when he grew up. They put a $10 bill on the dining room table; that would represent a banker. Next to the bill, they put a new Bible; that would represent a minister. Beside the Bible, they put a bottle of whiskey; that would represent a bum. The couple hid where they could watch their son without being seen.

Presently, the boy walked into the dining room, and immediately noticed the items on the table. He looked around carefully, then picked up the money, held it up to the light, then put it down again. He picked up the Bible, thumbed through it, and put that down, too. Then he quickly uncapped the whiskey bottle and sniffed the contents. In one rapid motion, he stuffed the $10 bill into his pocket, put the Bible under his arm, chugged down the contents of the bottle, and went whistling out of the room.

"Well, that settles that," the man said to his wife. "He's going to be a lawyer."

A doctor and a lawyer in two cars collided on a country road.

The lawyer, seeing that the doctor was a little shaken up, helped him from the car and offered him a drink from his hip flask.

The doctor accepted and handed the flask back to the lawyer, who closed it and put it away.

"Aren't you going to have a drink yourself?" asked the doctor.

"Sure, after the police leave," replied the lawyer.

Two lawyers walking through the woods spotted a vicious-looking bear.

The first lawyer immediately opened his briefcase, pulled out a pair of sneakers, and started putting them on.

The second lawyer looked at him and said, "You're crazy! You'll never be able to outrun that bear!"

"I don't have to," the first lawyer replied. "I only have to outrun you."

How can you tell when a lawyer is lying?

His lips are moving.

A lawyer had a leaking faucet in his office bathroom. He got the number of a nearby plumber and called him in.

The plumber arrived, and within five minutes, dismantled and repaired the faucet. Washing his hands, the plumber told the lawyer, "That will be a hundred and fifty dollars."

"What? That's outrageous!" replied the lawyer. "Why, that's more money than I make in an hour."

"I know," the plumber said. "That's why I quit being a lawyer."

A large cosmetics company posted the following notice in their laboratory:

Due to the great increase of actions by PETA and other animal rights advocates against testing cosmetics on rats, our laboratory will immediately begin to use lawyers to test our products.

The reasons for this change are as follows:

1) There is no shortage of lawyers.

2) Lab technicians won't get too attached to them.

3) There are things you simply can't get a rat to do.

A young guy walks into a post office one day to see a middle-aged, balding man standing at the counter methodically placing "Love" stamps on bright pink envelopes with hearts all over them. He then takes out a perfume bottle and starts spraying scent all over them.

His curiosity getting the better of him, he goes up to the balding man and asks him what he is doing. The man says, "I'm sending out a thousand Valentine cards signed, 'Guess who?' "

"But why?" asks the young man.

"I'm a divorce lawyer," the other man replies.

What is the difference between a tick and a lawyer?

A tick falls off of you when you die.

Mr. Graham was the chairman of the United Way. One day it came to his attention that the fund had never received a donation from the most successful lawyer in town. He called on the attorney. "Our research shows that you made a profit of over six hundred thousand dollars last year, and yet you have not given a dime to the community charities. What do you have to say for yourself?"

The lawyer replied, "Did your research also show that my mother is dying after a long illness, and has medical bills that are several times her annual income? Did your research uncover anything about my brother, the disabled veteran, who is blind and in a wheelchair? Do you know about my sister, whose husband died in a traffic accident, leaving her penniless with three children?"

Sheepishly, the charity solicitor admitted that he had no knowledge of any of this.

"Well, since I don't give any money to them, why should I give any to you?"

A man sat down at a bar, looked into his shirt pocket, and ordered a double scotch. A few minutes later, the man again peeked into his pocket and ordered another double.

This routine was followed for some time, until after looking into his pocket, he told the bartender that he'd had enough. The bartender said, "I've got to ask you: Why do you keep looking in your pocket?"

The man replied, "I have my lawyer's picture in there. When he starts to look honest, I know I've had enough."

Lawyer's creed: A man is innocent until proven broke.

A man walked into a lawyer's office and inquired about the lawyer's rates.

"Fifty dollars for three questions," replied the lawyer.

"Isn't that awfully steep?" asked the man.

"Yes," the lawyer replied, "and what was your third question?"

Why don't lawyers go to the beach?

Cats keep trying to bury them in the sand.

How do you save a drowning lawyer?

Take your foot off his head.

What's the difference between a lawyer and a vampire?

A vampire sucks blood only at night.

If you see a lawyer on a bicycle, why shouldn't you swerve and hit him?

It might be your bicycle.

What does a lawyer use for birth control?

His personality.

What is the ideal weight of a lawyer?

About three pounds, including the urn.

What did the terrorist who hijacked a jumbo jet full of lawyers do?

He threatened to release one every hour if his demands weren't met.

What's the difference between a lawyer and a vulture?

Vultures can't take their wing tips off.

Why are lawyers never attacked by sharks?

Professional courtesy.

An engineer, a physicist, and a lawyer were being interviewed for a position as chief executive officer of a large corporation. The engineer was interviewed first and was asked a long list of questions, ending with, "How much is two plus two?"

The engineer excused himself and made a series of measurements and calculations before returning to the board room and announcing, "Four."

The physicist was interviewed next and was asked the same questions. Again, the last question was, "How much is two plus two?"

Before answering the last question, he excused himself, made for the library, and did a great deal of research. After consulting with the United States Bureau of Standards and making many calculations, he also announced, "Four."

The lawyer was interviewed last, and again the final question was, "How much is two plus two?"

The lawyer drew all the shades in the room, looked outside to see if anyone was there, checked the telephone for listening devices, and finally whispered, "How much do you want it to be?"

Why are there so many toxic dump sites in New Jersey and so many lawyers in Washington?

New Jersey had first choice.

What's brown and white and looks good on pinstripes?

A pit bull attacking a lawyer.

The American writer Ambrose Bierce used to define a lawsuit as "a machine which you go into as a pig and come out of as a sausage."

He went on to define a lawyer as "one skilled in circumvention of the law." And a liar: "A lawyer with a roving commission."

There were three men traveling together: a priest, a farmer, and a lawyer.

It was starting to get late, and they needed to find a place to sleep. At last, they came across a farm. They stopped and asked the farmer there if they could spend the night.

He said, "That's fine, but my guest room is only big enough for two people. One of you will have to sleep in the barn."

The priest said, "I don't mind sleeping with God's creatures. I will take the barn."

They all agreed and went to their rooms.

About an hour later, there was a knock at the guest room door, and there stood the priest. "There is a chicken in there that won't stop clucking! I'm sorry, but I'm going to have to sleep in the guest room."

"That's okay," said the farmer, "I'll sleep in the barn. After all, I'm used to it."

So they all agreed and traded places.

About an hour later, there was a knock at the guest room door, and there stood the farmer. "I can't stand the smell from that cow in there anymore. I'm sorry, but I'm going to have to sleep in the guest room."

"Well, I guess that leaves me," said the lawyer. So he went to sleep in the barn. About an hour later, there was a knock at the guest room door, and there stood the chicken and the cow.

What do you need when you have three lawyers up to their necks in cement?

More cement.

A doctor told a rich old man that he would surely die if he didn't get a new heart soon.

The old man told the doctor to search the world for the best heart available, and that money was no object.

A few days later the doctor called the old man to tell him he had found three hearts, but that they were all expensive.

The old man reminded the doctor that he was filthy rich and implored him to tell him about the heart donors.

"Well," the doctor began, "the first one belonged to a twenty-two-year-old marathon runner who never smoked, ate only the healthiest foods, and was in peak condition when he was hit by a bus. No damage to the heart, of course. But it costs a hundred thousand dollars!"

The old man waved off the last part about the cost and asked the doctor to tell him about the second donor.

"This one belonged to a sixteen-year-old long-distance swimmer, high school kid. Lean and mean. Drowned when he hit his head on the side of a swimming pool. That heart'll set you back a hundred and fifty thousand!"

"Okay," said the old man, "what about the third heart?"

"Well, that one belonged to a fifty-eight-year-old man who smoked three packs of cigarettes a day, weighed over three hundred pounds, never exercised, drank like a fish. That heart is going for five hundred thousand!"

"Five hundred grand?!" the old man exclaimed, "Why so expensive?"

"Well," said the doctor, "this heart belonged to a lawyer . . . so it was never used!"

What's the difference between a lawyer and a bucket of dirt?

The bucket.

Why are lawyers buried ten feet under ground?

Because deep down under, they're really not that bad.

What's the difference between a lawyer and a snake?

When you run over a snake, you don't back up to make sure it's dead.

What is the difference between a lawyer and a sperm cell?

The sperm cell has one-in-a-million chance of becoming a human being.

A client asked his lawyer what he would charge for taking on his case.

After pondering the merits and problems of the case, the lawyer replied that he would take the case on a contingency fee.

"What's a contingency fee?" the client asked.

"A contingency fee means that if I don't win your suit, I don't get anything. And if I do win your suit, you don't get anything."

At the conclusion of the trial, the jury found the defendant Howard Billingsly not guilty. His lawyer congratulated him, then handed him a bill.

Billingsly looked at the bill and gulped. "This says I have to pay ten thousand dollars now and five hundred a month for the next five years! It sounds like I'm buying a Mercedes-Benz!"

The lawyer smiled. "You are."

How do you tell whether it's a skunk or a lawyer that's been run over on the highway?

There are skid marks around the skunk.

A woman was diagnosed with a brain tumor and was told that she needed to have a one-pound brain transplant. Her doctor asked her what kind of brain she wanted.

"I have a choice?" she asked, astonished.

"Yes," replied the doctor. "But there's a substantial

difference in price. For example, the one-pound brain of a surgeon costs sixty thousand dollars, while the one-pound brain of a truck driver goes for twenty thousand."

The woman thought for a moment and asked, "Can you get me the one-pound brain of a lawyer? I've always wanted to be a trial attorney."

"Yes, but it will cost you two hundred fifty thousand."

"Why so much, Doctor?"

"Do you have any idea how many lawyers it takes to produce a pound of brain?"

A dying man gathered his lawyer, doctor, and clergyman at his bedside and handed each of them an envelope containing $25,000 in cash. He made them each promise that after his death and during his repose, they would place the three envelopes in his coffin. He told them that he wanted to have enough money to enjoy the next life.

A week later, the man died. At the wake, one by one the lawyer, doctor, and clergyman concealed an envelope in the coffin and bid their old client and friend farewell.

By chance, these three met several months later. Soon the clergyman, feeling guilty, confessed that there was only $10,000 in the envelope he placed in the coffin. He felt, rather than waste all the money, he would send it to a mission in South America. He asked for their forgiveness.

The doctor, moved by the gentle clergyman's sincerity, confessed that he too had kept some of the money for a worthy medical charity. The envelope, he admitted, had only $8,000 in it. He said that he too could not bring himself to waste the money so frivolously when it could be used to benefit others.

By this time, the lawyer was seething with self-righteous outrage. He expressed his deep disappointment in the felonious behavior of two of his oldest and most trusted friends. "I am the only one who kept his promise to our dying friend," he told them. "I want you both to know that the envelope I placed in the coffin contained the full amount. Indeed, my envelope contained my personal check for the entire twenty-five thousand."

Lightbulb Jokes

The first is the great-great-grandfather of all lightbulb jokes; various ethnic groups perceived as stupid have been substituted for "morons" over the years:

How many morons does it take to screw in a lightbulb?

Five: One to hold the bulb in the socket, and four to rotate the moron.

How many Irishmen does it take to change a lightbulb?

Twenty-one: One to hold the bulb, and twenty to drink until the room spins.

How many blondes does it take to screw in a lightbulb?

What's a lightbulb?

How many feminists does it take to screw in a lightbulb?

That's not funny.

How many Teamsters does it take to change a lightbulb?

Fifty-three. You got a problem with that, buddy?

How many Christians does it take to screw in a lightbulb?

Three, but they're really one.

How many Jews does it take to screw in a lightbulb?

Three: One to call the cleaning lady, and two to feel guilty about it.

How many Catholics does it take to screw in a lightbulb?

Two: One to do it, and a priest to hear him confess and give the old bulb last rites.

How many Zen masters does it take to change a lightbulb?

Two: One to do it, and one not to.

How many EST followers does it take to screw in a lightbulb?

Fifty. Everybody takes turns trying to screw it in while the leader tells them all what rotten bulb screwers they are. No one is allowed to go to the bathroom during the entire procedure.

How many missionaries does it take to screw in a lightbulb?

One, and thirty natives to see the light.

How many small-town people does it take to screw in a lightbulb?

Two: One to do it, and a cop to make sure he isn't doing it too fast.

How many suburbanites does it take to screw in a lightbulb?

One, but it has to look like every other lightbulb on the block.

How many social scientists does it take to change a lightbulb?

They do not change lightbulbs. They search for the root cause as to why the last one went out.

How many psychiatrists does it take to change a lightbulb?

Just one. But it takes a long time, and the bulb really has to want to change.

How many paranoids does it take to change a lightbulb?

Who wants to know?

How many accountants does it take to screw in a lightbulb?

What kind of answer did you have in mind?

How many carpenters does it take to screw in a lightbulb?

Screw you! That's the electrician's job.

How many art museum visitors does it take to screw in a lightbulb?

Two: One to do it, and one to say, "My four-year-old could do that."

How many homeowners does it take to screw in a lightbulb?

Only one, but it takes him two weekends and three trips to the hardware store.

How many actors does it take to change a lightbulb?

Only one. They don't like to share the spotlight.

How many poets does it take to screw in a lightbulb?

Two: One to curse the darkness, and one to light a candle.

How many musicians does it take to screw in a lightbulb?

Eighteen: One to do it, and seventeen to be in on the guest list.

How many folk musicians does it take to screw in a lightbulb?

Forty: One to do it, and thirty-nine to complain that it's electric.

How many country musicians does it take to screw in a lightbulb?

Five: One to do it, and four to sing about how much they're going to miss the old one.

How many jugglers does it take to screw in a lightbulb?

One, but he uses at least three bulbs.

How many aides does it take to change President Reagan's lightbulb?

None, they like to keep him in the dark.

How many generals does it take to screw in a lightbulb?

None, they can all see by the light at the end of the tunnel.

How many bikers does it take a change a lightbulb?

It takes two. One to change the bulb, and the other to kick the switch.

How many college football players does it take to change a lightbulb?

The entire team, and they all get three credits each for it.

How many recovering addicts does it take to screw in a lightbulb?

Two: One to screw it in, and one to sponsor him.

How many blind people does it take to change a lightbulb?

It depends whether the switch is on or off.

How many dyslexics does it take to bulb a light change?

Eno.

How many bureaucrats/civil servants does it take to screw in a lightbulb?

Two: One to assure everyone that everything possible is being done, while the other screws the bulb into the water faucet.

How many existentialists does it take to change a lightbulb?

Two: One to screw it in, and another to observe how the lightbulb itself symbolizes a single incandescent beacon of subjective reality in a netherworld of endless absurdity reaching out toward a maudlin cosmos of nothingness.

How many military information officers does it take to change a lightbulb?

At the present point in time it is against policy and the best interests of military strategy to divulge information of such a statistical nature. Next question, please.

How many socialists does it take to change a lightbulb?

One to petition the Ministry of Light for a bulb, fifty to establish the state production quota, two hundred militia to force the factory unions to allow production of the bulb, and one to surreptitiously dial an 800 number to order an American lightbulb.

How many environmentalists does it take to change a lightbulb?

If the lightbulb is out, that's the way nature intended it!

How many Christian Scientists does it take to screw in a lightbulb?

None, but it takes at least one to sit and pray for the old one to go back on.

How many liberals does it take to screw in a lightbulb?

Five: One to screw it in, and four to screw it up.

How many conservatives does it take to change a lightbulb?

Four: One to do it, and three to complain that the old bulb was a lot better.

How many Libertarians does it take to screw in a lightbulb?

None, because somebody might come into the room who likes to sit in the dark.

How many dysfunctional family members does it take to screw in a lightbulb?

Lightbulb? What lightbulb?

How many consultants does it take to change a lightbulb?

Unknown. They never get past the feasibility study.

How many NASA technicians does it take to change a lightbulb?

Seventy, and they plan it for two weeks, and when they finally get around to it the weather's bad so they postpone it till next week. The lightbulb costs 3 million dollars.

How many Californians does it take to change a lightbulb?

Six: One to turn the bulb, one for support, and four to relate to the experience.

How many Oregonians does it take to screw in a lightbulb?

Five. One to change the bulb, and four more to chase off the Californians who have come up to relate to the experience.

How many software people does it take to screw in a lightbulb?

None. That's a hardware problem.

How many hardware folks does it take to change a lightbulb?

None. They just have marketing portray the dead bulb as a feature.

How many graduate students does it take to screw in a lightbulb?

Only one, but it may take upward of five years for him to get it done.

How many Russian leaders does it take to change a lightbulb?

Nobody knows. Russian leaders don't last as long as lightbulbs.

How many surrealists does it take to change a lightbulb?

Two: One to hold the giraffe, and the other to fill the bathtub with brightly colored machine tools.

How many doctors does it take to screw in a lightbulb?

Three: One to find a bulb specialist, one to find a bulb installation specialist, and one to bill it all to Medicare.

How many lawyers does it take to change a lightbulb?

How many can you afford?

How many federal employees does it take to screw in a lightbulb?

Sorry, that item has been cut from the budget!

How many "pro-lifers" does it take to change a lightbulb?

Six: Two to screw in the bulb, and four to testify that it was lit from the moment they began screwing.

How many sorority sisters does it take to change a lightbulb?

Fifty-one. One to change the bulb, and fifty to sing about the bulb being changed.

How many frat guys does it take to screw in a lightbulb?

Three: One to screw it in, and the other two to help him down off the keg.

How many necrophiliacs does it take to screw in a lightbulb?

None. Necrophiliacs prefer dead bulbs.

How many dadaists does it take to screw in a lightbulb?

To get to the other side.

How many Chernobylians does it take to screw in a lightbulb?

None. People who glow in the dark don't need lightbulbs.

How many magicians does it take to change a lightbulb?
Depends on what you want to change it into.

How many nihilists does it take to change a lightbulb?
There is nothing to change.

Miscellaneous

Toward the end of World War II, a humorous "Indoctrination for Return of Army Soldiers to the U.S." was fairly widely circulated. Here are excerpts:

SUBJECT: Indoctrination for Return to U.S.
TO: All Units

A. In compliance with current policies for rotation of armed forces overseas it is directed that in order to maintain the high standard of character of the American soldier and to prevent any dishonor to reflect on the uniform, all individuals eligible for return to the U.S. under current directives will undergo an indoctrination course of demilitarization prior to approval of his application for return.

B. The following points will be emphasized in the subject indoctrination course:

1. In America there is a remarkable number of beautiful girls. These young ladies have not been liberated and many are gainfully employed as stenographers, salesgirls, beauty operators, or welders. Contrary to current practice they should not be approached with, "How much?" A proper greeting is, "Isn't it a lovely day?" or "Have you ever been to Chicago?" Then say, "How much?"
2. A guest in a private home is usually awakened in the morning by a light tapping on his door, and an invitation to join the host at breakfast. It is proper to say, "I'll be there shortly." DO NOT say, "Blow it out your—."
3. A typical American breakfast consists of such strange foods as cantaloupes, fresh eggs, milk, ham, etc. These are highly palatable and, though strange in appearance, extremely tasty. Butter, made from cream, is often served. If you wish for some butter, you turn to the person nearest it and say quietly, "Please pass the butter." DO NOT say, "Throw me the goddamned grease."
4. Very natural urges are apt to occur when in a crowd. If it is found necessary to defecate, one does NOT grab a shovel in one hand and paper in the other and run for the garden. At least 90 percent of American homes have one room called a "bathroom," i.e., a room that, in most cases, contains a bathtub, washbasin, medicine cabinet, and

a toilet. It is the latter that you will use in this case. (Instructors should make sure that all personnel understand the operation of the toilet, particularly the lever or button arrangement that serves to prepare the device for reuse.)

5. In the event the helmet is retained by the individual, he will refrain from using it as a chair, washbowl, footbath, or bathtub. All these devices are furnished in the average American home. It is not considered good practice to squat Indian fashion in a corner in the event all chairs are occupied. The host usually will provide suitable seats.

6. American dinners, in most cases, consist of several items, each served in a separate dish. The common practice of mixing various items, such as corned beef and pudding, or lima beans and peaches, to make them more palatable will be refrained from. In time the "separate dish" system will become enjoyable.

7. Americans have a strange taste for stimulants. The drinks in common usage on the Continent, such as underripe wine, alcohol and grapefruit juice, or gasoline bitters and water (commonly known by the French as "Cognac") are not usually acceptable in civilian circles. A suitable use for such drinks is for serving one's landlord in order to break an undesirable lease.

8. In traveling in the U.S., particularly in a strange city, it is often necessary to spend the night. Hotels are provided for this purpose, and almost any-

one can give directions to the nearest hotel. Here, for a small sum, you can register and be shown to a room where you can sleep for the night. The present practice of entering the nearest house, throwing the occupants into the yard, and taking over the premises will cease.

9. Whiskey, a common American drink, may be offered to the soldier on social occasions. It is considered a reflection on the uniform to snatch the bottle from the hostess and drain the bottle, cork and all. All individuals are cautioned to exercise extreme control in these circumstances.

10: In motion picture theaters seats are provided. Helmets are not required. It is NOT considered good form to whistle every time a female over eight and under eighty crosses the screen. If vision is impaired by the person in the seat in front, there are plenty of other seats that can be occupied. DO NOT hit him across the back of the head and say, "Move your head, jerk, I can't see a damn thing."

11. Upon retiring, one will often find a pair of pajamas laid out on the bed. (Pajamas, it should be explained, are two-piece garments that are donned after all clothing has been removed.) The soldier, confronted by these garments, should assume an air of familiarity and not act as though he were not used to them. A casual remark such as, "My, what a delicate shade of blue" will usually suffice. Under NO circumstances say, "How

in hell do you expect me to sleep in a getup like that?"

12. Beer is sometimes served in bottles. A cap remover is usually available, and it is not good form to open the bottle by the use of one's teeth.
13. Always tip your hat before striking a lady.
14. Air raids and enemy patrols are not encountered in America. Therefore it is not necessary to wear the helmet in church or at social gatherings, or to hold the weapon at ready, loaded and cocked, when talking to civilians in the street.
15. Every American home and all hotels are equipped with bathing facilities. When one desires to take a bath, it is not considered good form to find the nearest pool or stream, strip down, and indulge in a bath. This is particularly true in heavily populated areas.
16. All individuals returning to the U.S. will make every effort to conform to the customs and habits of the regions visited, and to make themselves as inconspicuous as possible. Any actions that reflect upon the honor of the uniform will be promptly dealt with.

A pollster was taking opinions outside the United Nations building in New York City. He approached four men waiting to cross the street: a Saudi, a Russian, a North Korean, and a resident New Yorker. He asked, "Excuse me, I would like to ask you your opinion on the current meat shortage?"

The Saudi replied, "Excuse me, but what is a shortage?"

The Russian said, "Excuse me, but what is meat?"

The North Korean replied, "Excuse me, but what is an opinion?"

The New Yorker replied, "What is 'excuse me'?"

For decades, two heroic statues, one male and one female, faced each other in a city park. One day, an angel came down from heaven and approached the statues.

"You've been such exemplary statues," the angel announced to them, "that I'm going to give you a special gift. I'm going to bring you both to life for thirty minutes, during which time you can do anything you want." And with a clap of his hands, the angel brought the statues to life.

The two approached each other a bit shyly, but soon dashed for the bushes, from which shortly emerged a good deal of giggling and shaking of branches. Fifteen minutes later, the two statues emerged from the bushes, wide grins on their faces.

"You still have fifteen more minutes," said the angel, winking at them.

Grinning widely, the female statue turned to the male statue and said, "Great! Only this time *you* hold down the pigeon and I'll crap on its head!"

Before going to Europe on business, a man drove his Rolls-Royce to a downtown New York City bank and went in to ask for an immediate loan of $5,000.

The loan officer, taken aback, requested collateral, and so the man said, "Well then, here are the keys to my Rolls-Royce."

The loan officer promptly had the car driven into the bank's underground parking for safekeeping, and gave him $5,000.

Two weeks later, the man walked through the bank's doors and asked to settle up his loan and get his car back. "That will be five thousand dollars in principal, and fifteen dollars and forty cents in interest," the loan officer said.

The man wrote out a check and started to walk away.

"Wait, sir," the loan officer said. "While you were gone, I found out you are a millionaire. Why in the world would you need to borrow five thousand dollars?"

The man smiled. "Where else could I park my Rolls-Royce in Manhattan for two weeks and pay only fifteen dollars and forty cents?"

The stockbroker was nervous about being in prison because his cell mate looked like a real thug.

"Don't worry," the gruff-looking fellow said, "I'm in here for a white-collar crime too."

"Well, that's a relief," said the stockbroker, sighing. "I was sent to prison for fraud and insider trading."

"Oh, nothing fancy like that for me." The convict grinned. "I just killed a couple of priests."

A man was sued by a woman for defamation of character. She charged that he had called her a pig. The man was found guilty and fined.

After the trial he asked the judge, "This means that I cannot call Mrs. Johnson a pig?"

The judge said that was true.

"Does this mean I cannot call a pig Mrs. Johnson?" the man asked.

The judge replied that he could indeed call a pig Mrs. Johnson with no fear of legal action.

The man looked directly at Mrs. Johnson and said, "Good afternoon, Mrs. Johnson."

A young man was walking through a supermarket to pick up a few things when he noticed an old lady following him around. Thinking nothing of it, he ignored her and continued on. Finally, he went to the checkout line, but she got in front of him.

"Pardon me," she said, "I'm sorry if my staring at you has made you feel uncomfortable. It's just that you look just like my son, whom I haven't seen in a long time."

"That's a shame," replied the young man. "Is there anything I can do for you?"

"Yes," she said, "as I'm leaving, can you say 'Good-bye, Mother!' It would make me feel so much better."

"Sure," answered the young man.

As the old woman was leaving, he called out, "Good-bye, Mother!"

As he stepped up to the checkout counter, he saw that his total was $127.50.

"How can that be?" he asked. "I purchased only a few things!"

"Your mother said that you would pay for her," said the clerk.

Three men were found in the wilderness by civilized cannibals. The men were led to a grave site next to the water. The chief told them, "We will kill you as cowards, or we will let you die honorable deaths. You choose the weapon. Either way, your skins will be used to make our canoes."

The first man, a soldier at heart, asked for a handgun, shot himself, and was carried off by the cannibals.

The next man asked for a sword. A warrior at heart, he committed seppuku as would a Japanese man. He, too, was carried off by the cannibals.

The last man asked for a fork.

"A fork?" asked the chief.

But it was his dying wish, so they handed him a fork. He stabbed himself repeatedly in the chest, and yelled, "I hope your canoe sinks!"

30 Politically Correct Ways to Say Someone Is Stupid

1. A few clowns short of a circus

2. A few fries short of a Happy Meal

3. An experiment in Artificial Stupidity

4. A few beers short of a six-pack

5. A few peas short of a casserole

6. Doesn't have all his cornflakes in one box
7. The wheel's spinning, but the hamster's dead
8. One Fruit Loop shy of a full bowl
9. One taco short of a combination plate
10. A few feathers short of a whole duck
11. All foam, no beer
12. Body by Fisher, brains by Mattel
13. Has an I.Q. of 2, but it takes 3 to grunt
14. Warning: Objects in mirror are dumber than they appear
15. Couldn't pour water out of a boot with instructions on the heel
16. Too much yardage between the goalposts
17. An intellect rivaled only by garden tools
18. As smart as bait
19. Doesn't have all his dogs on one leash
20. Doesn't know much, but leads the league in nostril hair
21. Elevator doesn't go all the way to the top floor
22. Forgot to pay his brain bill
23. Her antenna doesn't pick up all the channels
24. His belt doesn't go through all the loops
25. If he had another brain, it would be lonely
26. No grain in the silo

27. Proof that evolution can go in reverse
28. Receiver is off the hook
29. Several nuts short of a full pouch
30. He fell out of the stupid tree and hit every branch on the way down

A graduate with a science degree asks, "Why does it work?"

A graduate with an engineering degree asks, "How does it work?"

A graduate with an accounting degree asks, "How much will it cost?"

A graduate with a liberal arts degree asks, "Do you want fries with that?"

A young woman was sitting on the bus cooing to her baby when a drunk staggered aboard and down the aisle. Stopping in front of her, he looked down and pronounced, "Lady, that is the ugliest baby I have ever seen."

The woman burst into tears, and there was such an outcry of sympathy among the other passengers that they kicked the drunk off. But the woman kept on sobbing and wailing so loudly that finally the driver pulled the bus over to the side of the road.

"Look, I don't know what that bum said to you," the driver told his inconsolable passenger, "but to help calm you down I'm going to get you a cup of tea." And off he went, coming back shortly with a cup of tea from the corner deli.

"Now calm down, lady," soothed the driver. "Everything's going to be okay. See, I brought you a cup of nice hot tea, and I even got a banana for your pet monkey."

"May I take your order?" the waiter asked.

"Yes. I'm just wondering, how do you prepare your chickens?"

"Nothing special sir," he replied. "We just tell them straight out that they're going to die."

The army sergeant called for his morning formation and lined up all the troops. "Listen up, men," said the sergeant. "Johnson, report to the mess hall for KP. Smith, report to Personnel to sign some papers. The rest of you men report to the motor pool for maintenance. Oh, by the way, Rudkin, your mother died, report to the commander."

Later that day, the captain called the sergeant into his office. "Hey, Sarge, that was a pretty cold way to inform Rudkin that his mother died. Could you be a bit more tactful next time?"

"Yes, sir," answered the sergeant.

A few months later, the captain called the sergeant in

again, saying, "Sarge, I just got a telegram that Private Fogle's mother died. You'd better go tell him, and send him in to see me. And this time, be more tactful."

So the sergeant called for his morning formation. "Okay, men, fall in and listen up. Everybody with a mother, take two steps forward. *Not so fast, Fogle!*"

A nice young worker from the post office was sorting through her regular envelopes when she discovered a letter addressed as follows:

GOD

c/o Heaven

Upon opening the envelope, the letter enclosed told about a little old lady who had never asked for anything in her life. She was desperately in need of $100 and was wondering if God could send her the money.

The young lady was deeply touched, and she passed the hat among her workmates. She managed to collect $90, and she sent it off to the old lady.

A few weeks later another letter arrived addressed in the same way to God, so the young lady opened it. The letter read, "Thank you for the money, God, I deeply appreciate it. However, I received only $90. It must have been those bastards at the post office."

Heaven is a place where:

The lovers are Italian

The cooks are French

The mechanics are German

The police are English

The government is run by the Swiss

Hell is a place where:

The lovers are Swiss

The cooks are English

The mechanics are French

The police are German

The government is run by the Italians

Here's How Some American Advertising Slogans Translate into Foreign Languages:

Coors translated its slogan "Turn It Loose" into Spanish, where it was read as "Suffer from Diarrhea."

Chicken magnate Frank Perdue's line, "It takes a tough man to make a tender chicken," sounds much more interesting in Spanish: "It takes a sexually stimulated man to make a chicken affectionate."

The Chevy Nova never sold well in Spanish-speaking countries. "No Va" means "It Does Not Go" in Spanish.

When Pepsi started marketing its products in

China a few years back, they translated their slogan, "Pepsi Brings You Back to Life" pretty literally. The slogan in Chinese really meant, "Pepsi Brings Your Ancestors Back from the Grave."

Then when Coca-Cola first shipped to China, they named the product something that when pronounced sounded like "Coca-Cola." The only problem was that the characters used meant "Bite the Wax Tadpole." They later changed to a set of characters that mean "Happiness in the Mouth."

When Gerber first started selling baby food in Africa, they used the same packaging as here in the United States, with the cute baby on the label—until they found out that in Africa, companies routinely put pictures on the label of what actually is inside the container since most people cannot read.

Jolly Green Giant translated into Arabic means "Intimidating Green Ogre."

A new business was opening, and one of the owner's friends sent flowers for the occasion. But when the owner read the card with the flowers, it said, "Rest in Peace."

The owner was a little peeved, and he called the florist to complain.

After he had told the florist about the obvious mistake, the florist said, "Sir, I'm really sorry for the mistake, but rather than getting angry, you should imagine this: Somewhere there is a funeral taking place today, and *they* have flowers with a note saying, "Congratulations on your new location."

During the French revolution, many hundreds of people were executed by guillotine. One day, three men were led up to die. One was a lawyer, one was a doctor, and the third was an engineer.

The lawyer was to die first. He was led to the guillotine, the attending priest blessed him, and he knelt with his head on the guillotine. The blade was released but stopped halfway down its path. The priest, seeing an opportunity, quickly said, "Gentlemen, God has spoken and said this man is to be spared; we cannot kill him." The executioner agreed, and the lawyer was set free.

The doctor was next. He was blessed by the priest, then knelt and placed his head down. The blade was released, and again stopped halfway down. Again the priest intervened: "Gentlemen, God has again spoken; we cannot kill this man." The executioner agreed, and the doctor was set free.

At last it was the engineer's turn. He was blessed by the priest and knelt, but before he placed his head on the guillotine, he looked up. Suddenly, he leaped to his feet and cried, "Oh, I see the problem!"

Murphy's Laws for Our Times

Trust everybody . . . then cut the cards.

Two wrongs are only the beginning.

If at first you don't succeed, destroy all evidence that you tried.

To succeed in politics, it is often necessary to rise above your principles.

Exceptions prove the rule . . . and wreck the budget.

Success always occurs in private, and failure in full view.

Quality assurance doesn't.

Exceptions always outnumber rules.

He who hesitates is probably right.

One child is not enough, but two children are far too many.

A clean tie attracts the soup of the day.

The hardness of the butter is in direct proportion to the softness of the bread.

The bag that breaks is the one with the eggs.

When there are sufficient funds in the checking account, checks take two weeks to clear. When there are insufficient funds, checks clear overnight.

The book you spent $20.95 for today will come out in paperback tomorrow.

The more an item costs, the farther you have to send it for repairs.

Never ask the barber if you need a haircut or a salesman if his is a good price.

If it says, "one size fits all," it doesn't fit anyone.

You never really learn to swear until you learn to drive.

The colder the X-ray table, the more of your body is required to be on it.

Love letters, business contracts, and money due to you always arrive three weeks late, whereas junk mail arrives the day it was sent.

When you drop change at a vending machine, the pennies will fall nearby, while all other coins will roll out of sight.

The severity of the itch is inversely proportional to your reach.

Experience is something you don't get until just after you need it.

Life can only be understood backward, but it must be lived forward.

Interchangeable parts aren't.

No matter which way you go, it's uphill and against the wind.

Work is accomplished by those employees who have not reached their level of incompetence.

Progress is made on alternative Fridays.

No one's life, liberty, or property is safe while the legislature is in session.

The hidden flaw never remains hidden.

As soon as the flight attendant serves the coffee, the airline encounters turbulence.

For every action, there is an equal and opposite criticism.

People who love sausage and respect the law should never watch either of them being made.

A conclusion is the place where you got tired of thinking.

When reviewing your notes for a test, the most important ones will be completely illegible.

A free agent is anything but.

The least-experienced fisherman always catches the biggest fish.

Never do card tricks for the group you play poker with.

The one item you want is never the one on sale.

An accountant is someone who knows the cost of everything and the value of nothing.

An auditor is someone who arrives after the battle and bayonets all the wounded.

A banker is a fellow who lends you his umbrella when the sun is shining and wants it back the minute it begins to rain. (Mark Twain)

An economist is an expert who will know tomorrow why the things he predicted yesterday didn't happen today.

A statistician is someone who is good with numbers but lacks the personality to be an accountant.

An actuary is someone who brings a fake bomb on a plane because that decreases the chances that there will be another bomb on the plane.

A programmer is someone who solves a problem you didn't know you had in a way you don't understand.

A mathematician is a blind man in a dark room looking for a black cat that isn't there.

A topologist is a man who doesn't know the difference between a coffee cup and a doughnut.

A lawyer is a person who writes a 10,000-word document and calls it a "brief."

A psychologist is a man who watches everyone else when a beautiful girl enters the room.

A professor is one who talks in someone else's sleep.

A schoolteacher is a disillusioned woman who used to think she liked children.

A consultant is someone who takes the watch off your wrist and tells you the time.

A diplomat is someone who can tell you to go to hell in such a way that you will look forward to the trip.

A man who lived in a block of apartments thought it might be raining, so he put his hand out the window to check for raindrops. As he did so, a glass eye fell into his hand.

He stuck his head out to look up to see where the eye came from just in time to see a young woman looking down.

"Is this yours?" he asked.

She said, "Yes, could you bring it up?" and the man agreed.

The woman, who turned out to be very attractive, was profuse in her thanks and offered the man a drink. Naturally, he agreed.

Shortly afterward she said, "I'm about to have dinner. There's plenty; would you like to join me?"

He readily accepted her offer, and both enjoyed a lovely meal. As the evening was drawing to a close the woman said, "I've had a marvelous evening. Would you like to stay the night?"

The man hesitated, then said, "Do you act like this with every man you meet?"

"No," she replied, "only those who catch my eye."

Here Are Some Accountant Jokes, New and Old:

What's an auditor?

Someone who arrives after the battle and bayonets all the wounded.

What's an accountant's idea of trashing his hotel room?

Refusing to fill out the guest comment card.

When does a person decide to become an accountant?

When he realizes he doesn't have the charisma to succeed as an undertaker.

What's the most wicked thing a group of young accountants can do?

Go into town and gang-audit someone.

What's the definition of an accountant?

Someone who solves a problem you didn't know you had in a way you don't understand.

What's an actuary?

An accountant without the sense of humor.

What do actuaries do to liven up their office party?

Invite an accountant.

My accountant told me that the only reason why my business is looking up is that it's flat on its back.

An accountant is having a hard time sleeping and goes to see his doctor.

"Doctor, I just can't get to sleep at night."

"Have you tried counting sheep?"

"That's the problem—I make a mistake and then spend three hours trying to find it."

Old accountants never die. They just lose their balance.

A young executive was leaving the office late one evening when he found the CEO standing in front of a shredder with a piece of paper in his hand.

"Listen," said the CEO, "this is a very sensitive and important document here, and my secretary has gone for the night. Can you make this thing work?"

"Certainly," said the young executive. He turned the machine on, inserted the paper, and pressed the start button.

"Excellent, excellent!" said the CEO as his paper disappeared inside the machine. "I just need one copy."

A survey of personnel executives at 200 of the Fortune 1,000 companies provided the following unbelievable but true examples of job applicant behavior.

"The reason the candidate was taking so long to respond to a question became apparent when he began to snore."

"When I asked the candidate to give a good example of the organizational skills she was boasting about, she said she was proud of her ability to pack her suitcase 'real neat' for her vacations."

"Why did [the applicant] go to college?" His reply: "To party and socialize."

"When I gave him my business card at the beginning of the interview, he immediately crumpled it and tossed it in the wastebasket."

"I received a résumé and letter that said that the recent high-school graduate wanted to earn $25 an hour—'and not a nickel less.' "

"[The applicant] had arranged for a pizza to be delivered to my office during a lunch-hour interview. I asked him not to eat it until later."

"[The applicant] said she had just graduated cum laude, but she had no idea what cum laude meant. However, she was proud of her grade point average. It was 2.1."

"[The applicant] insisted on telling me that he wasn't afraid of hard work. But insisted on adding he was afraid of horses and didn't like jazz, modern art, or seafood."

"She actually showed up for an interview during the summer wearing a bathing suit. She said she didn't think I'd mind."

"He sat down opposite me, made himself comfortable, and proceeded to put his foot up on my desk."

"The interview had gone well, until he told me that he and his friends wore my company's clothing whenever they could. I had to tell him that we manufactured office products, not sportswear."

"[The applicant] applied for a customer service position, although, as he confided, he really wasn't a people person."

"Without asking if I minded, he casually lit a cigar and then tossed the match onto my carpet—and couldn't understand why I was upset."

"On the phone, I had asked the candidate to bring his résumé and a couple of references. He arrived with the résumé—and two people."

Our Town Is So Small That . . .

Our city limits signs are both on the same post.

The city jail is called amoeba, because it has only one cell.

The McDonald's has only one Golden Arch.

The 7-11 is a 3½-5½.

The one-block-long Main Street dead ends in both directions.

The phone book has only one page.

The ZIP code is a fraction.

Second Street is in the next town over.

A night on the town takes about eleven minutes.

The mayor had to annex property to eat a foot-long hot dog.

An exhausted hunter out in the wilds stumbled into a camp. "Am I glad to see you," he said. "I've been lost for three days."

"Don't get too excited, friend," the other hunter replied. "I've been lost for three weeks."

Some Amusing Things to Do in a Crowded Elevator

Smack your forehead and mutter: "Shut up! Shut up! All of you just shut up!"

Crack open your briefcase or purse, peer inside, and ask, "Got enough air in there?"

Stand silently and motionless in the corner, facing the wall, without getting off.

Stare, grinning, at another passenger for a while, then announce: "I've got new socks on."

Meow occasionally.

Bet the other passengers you can fit a quarter in your nose.

Stare at another passenger for a while, then announce: "You're one of them." Then move to the far corner of the elevator.

Walk on with an appropriately sized cooler that says "human head" on the side.

Wear a child's puppet on your hand and use it to talk to other passengers.

Say "Ding" at each floor.

Draw a little square on the floor with chalk and announce to the other passengers that this is your "personal space."

Announce in a demonic voice: "I must find a more suitable host body."

Make explosion noises when anyone presses a button.

A recent study found that 90 million people in the United States are illiterate. Twenty-five percent can't speak En-

glish. Here are a few key questions to determine if you are illiterate:

1. Do you own or manage a convenience store?
2. Was your life shattered when *The Dukes of Hazzard* went off the air?
3. Are you from Arkansas?
4. Have you ever considered pro wrestling as a viable career option?

Very Short Books

A Guide to Arab Democracies

A Journey through the Mind of Dennis Rodman

Amelia Earhart's Guide to the Pacific Ocean

Career Opportunities for History Majors

Detroit—A Travel Guide

Different Ways to Spell "Bob"

Dr. Kevorkian's Collection of Motivational Speeches

Ethiopian Tips on World Dominance

Everything Men Know About Women

French Hospitality

Bob Dole: The Wild Years

How to Sustain a Musical Career by Art Garfunkel

Mike Tyson's Guide to Dating Etiquette

Mormon Divorce Lawyers

One Hundred and One Spotted Owl Recipes by the EPA

Popular Lawyers

Staple Your Way to Success

Deep Questions

Do infants enjoy infancy as much as adults enjoy adultery?

How is it possible to have a civil war?

If all the world is a stage, where is the audience sitting?

If love is blind, why is lingerie so popular?

If one synchronized swimmer drowns, do the rest have to drown too?

If work is so terrific, how come they have to pay you to do it?

If you're born again, do you have two belly buttons?

If you ate pasta and antipasta, would you still be hungry?

If you try to fail, and succeed, which have you done?

Why is it called tourist season if we can't shoot at them?

Why is the alphabet in that order? Is it because of that song?

What happens when none of your bees wax?

If the black box flight recorder is never damaged during a plane crash, why isn't the whole airplane made out of the stuff?

Why is there an expiration date on sour cream?

If most car accidents occur within five miles of home, why doesn't everyone just move ten miles away?

Did you hear about the dyslexic devil worshiper?
He sold his soul to Santa.

A man piloting a hot-air balloon discovers he has wandered far off course and is hopelessly lost.

He descends to a lower altitude and locates a man down on the ground. He lowers the balloon to within hearing distance and shouts, "Excuse me, can you tell me where I am?"

The man below says: "Yes, you're in a hot-air balloon, about thirty feet above this field."

"You must work in information technology," says the balloonist.

"Yes, I do," replies the man. "And how did you know that?"

"Well," says the balloonist, "what you told me is technically correct, but of no use to anyone."

The man below says, "You must work in management."

"I do," replies the balloonist, "how did you know?"

"Well," says the man, "you don't know where you are, or where you're going, but you expect my immediate help. You're in the same position you were before we met, but now it's my fault!"

An explorer in the deepest Amazon suddenly finds himself surrounded by a bloodthirsty group of natives. Upon surveying the situation, he says quietly to himself, "Oh, God, I'm screwed."

The sky darkens, and a voice booms out, "No, you are *not* screwed. Pick up that stone at your feet and bash in the head of the chief standing in front of you."

So with the stone he bashes the life out of the chief. Standing above the lifeless body, breathing heavily, he looks at a hundred angry natives. . . .

The voice booms out again, "Okay . . . *now* you're screwed."

A middle-aged woman had a heart attack. Then, while on the operating table, she had a near-death experience. She saw God and asked if this was the end.

God said no, that she had another thirty to forty years to live.

Sure enough, she recovered, and decided to remain in the hospital to have a face-lift, liposuction, a tummy tucks her hair dyed—the works. She figured since she had another thirty or forty years, she might as well make the most of it.

She walked out of the hospital after the last operation and was immediately hit by an ambulance.

She arrived before God and whined, "I thought you said I had another thirty or forty years."

God replied, "To tell you the truth, I didn't recognize you."

Two guys were bungee jumping one day. The first guy said to the second. "You know, we could make a lot of money running our own bungee-jumping service in Mexico."

The second guy thought this was a great idea, so the two pooled their money and bought everything they'd need—a tower, an elastic cord, insurance, and so forth.

They traveled to Mexico and began to set up on the square of a small town. As they constructed the tower, a crowd began to assemble. Slowly, more and more people gathered to watch them at work.

At last, the tower and the bungee cord were ready. The first guy jumped. He bounced at the end of the cord, but when he came back up, the second guy noticed that he had a few cuts and scratches. Unfortunately, the second guy wasn't able catch him; he fell again, bounced, and came back up again. That time he was bruised and bleeding. Again, the second guy couldn't catch him, and the first guy fell again and bounced back up. That time, he came back pretty messed up, with a couple of broken bones and nearly unconscious.

Luckily, the second guy finally caught him. "What happened?" he cried. "Was the cord too long?"

The first guy said, "No, the cord was fine, but what the heck is a 'piñata'?"

Without warning, a hurricane blew across the Caribbean. The luxurious yacht soon foundered in the huge waves and sank without a trace. Only two survivors, the boat's owner and its steward, managed to swim to the closest island. Observing that it was utterly uninhabited, the steward burst into tears, wringing his hands and moaning that they'd never be heard of again. Meanwhile, his companion leaned back against a palm tree and relaxed.

"Dr. Karpman, how can you be so calm?" moaned the distraught steward. "We're going to die on this godforsaken island. They're never going to find us."

"Let me tell you something, Mitchell," began Karpman with a smile. "Four years ago I gave five hundred thousand dollars to the United Way, and five hundred thousand dollars to the United Jewish Appeal. Three years ago I did very well in the stock market, so I contributed eight hundred and fifty thousand to each. Last year business was good, so both charities got a million dollars."

"So?" screamed the wretched steward.

"It's time for their annual fund drives," the yachtsman pointed out, "and I know they're going to find me."

A fellow was sitting in the doctor's waiting room, and he said to himself every so often, "Lord, I hope I'm sick!"

After about the fifth or sixth utterance, the receptionist couldn't stand it any longer and asked, "Why in the world would you want to be sick, Mr. Adams?"

The man replied, "Well, I'd hate to be well and feel like this."

The worried housewife sprang to the telephone when it rang and listened with relief to the kindly voice in her ear.

"How are you, darling?" it said. "What kind of a day are you having?"

"Oh, Mother," said the housewife, breaking into bitter tears, "I've had such a bad day. The baby won't eat, and the washing machine broke down. I haven't had a chance to go shopping, and besides, I've just sprained my ankle, and I have to hobble around. On top of that, the house is a mess, and I'm supposed to have two couples to dinner tonight."

The mother was shocked and was at once all sympathy. "Oh, darling," she said, "sit down, relax, and close your eyes. I'll be over in half an hour. I'll do your shopping, clean up the house, and cook your dinner for you. I'll feed the baby, and I'll call a repairman I know who'll be at your house to fix the washing machine promptly. Now stop crying. I'll do everything. In fact, I'll even call George at the office and tell him he ought to come home and help out for once."

"George?" said the housewife. "Who's George?"

"Why, George! Your husband! . . . Is this 555-1374?"

"No, this is 555-1375."

"Oh, I'm sorry. I guess I have the wrong number."

There was a short pause, and the housewife said, "Does this mean you're not coming over?"

A guy returns from a long trip to Europe, having left his beloved cat in his brother's care. The minute he clears customs, he calls his brother and inquires after his pet.

"The cat's dead," his brother replies bluntly.

The guy is devastated. "You don't know how much the cat meant to me," he sobs into the phone. "Couldn't you at least have given a little thought to a nicer way of breaking the news? For instance, couldn't you have said, 'Well, you know, the cat got out of the house one day and climbed up on the roof, and the fire department couldn't get her down, and finally she died of exposure . . . of starvation . . . or something'? Why are you always so thoughtless?"

"Look, I'm really, really sorry," says his brother. "I'll try to do better next time, I swear."

"Okay, let's just put it behind us. How are you, anyway? How's Mom?"

There was a long pause. "Uh," the brother finally stammers, "uh . . . Mom's on the roof."

7 Fun Things to Do in a Mall

1. Ask a salesman why a particular TV is labeled black and white and insist that it's a color set. When he

disagrees, give him a strange look and say, "You mean you really can't see it?"

2. If you're patient, stare intently into a surveillance camera for an hour while rocking from side to side.
3. Sprint up the down escalator.
4. Ask a salesperson in the hardware department how well a particular saw cuts through bone.
5. At the pet store, ask if they have bulk discounts on gerbils, and whether there's much meat on them.
6. Rummage through the jelly-bean bin at the candy store, insisting that you lost a contact lens.
7. In the changing rooms, announce in a singsong voice, "I see London, I see France. . . ."

Walking through Chinatown, a tourist was fascinated by all the Chinese restaurants, shops, and signs. He turned a corner and saw a building with the sign, "Lars Olaffsen's Laundry."

"Lars Olaffsen?" he mused. "How the heck does that fit in here?" So he walks into the shop and sees an old Chinese gentleman behind the counter.

The tourist asked, "How did this place get the name 'Lars Olffsen's Laundry?' "

The old man answered, "Is name of owner."

The tourist pressed further. "Well, who and where is the owner?"

"Me, is right here," replied the old man.

"You? How did you ever get a name like Lars Olaffsen?"

"Is simple," says the old man. "Many many year ago when come to this country, was stand in line at Documentation Center. Man in front was big blond Swede. Lady look at him and go, 'What your name?' He say, 'Lars Olaffsen.' Then she look at me and go, 'What your name?' I say, 'Sem Ting.' "

The day after a man lost his wife in a scuba diving accident, he was greeted by two grim-faced policemen at his door.

"We're sorry to call on you at this hour, Mr. Wilkens, but we have some information about your wife."

"Well, tell me!" the man said.

The policeman said, "We have some bad news, some good news, and some really great news. Which do you want to hear first?"

Fearing the worst, Mr. Wilkens said, "Give me the bad news first."

The policeman said, "I'm sorry to tell you, sir, but this morning we found your wife's body in San Francisco Bay."

"Oh my God!" said Mr. Wilkens, overcome by emotion. Then, remembering what the policeman had said, he asked, "What's the good news?"

"Well," said the policeman, "when we pulled her up she had two five-pound lobsters and a dozen good-size Dungeoness crabs on her."

"If that's the good news than what's the great news?" Mr. Wilkens demanded.

The policeman said, "We're going to pull her up again tomorrow morning."

Favorite Oxymorons

1. Act naturally
2. Found missing
3. Resident alien
4. Genuine imitation
5. Airline food
6. Good grief
7. Same difference
8. Almost exactly
9. Government organization
10. Sanitary landfill
11. Alone together
12. Legally drunk
13. Silent scream
14. American history
15. Living dead
16. Small crowd
17. Business ethics
18. Soft rock

19. Military intelligence
20. Sweet sorrow
21. Synthetic natural gas
22. Passive aggression
23. Taped live
24. Clearly misunderstood
25. Extinct life
26. Temporary tax increase
27. Terribly pleased
28. Computer security
29. Political science
30. Tight slacks
31. Pretty ugly
32. Twelve-ounce pound cake
33. Working vacation
34. Exact estimate

On the first day of college, the dean addressed the students, pointing out some of the rules:

"The female dormitory will be out-of-bounds for all male students, and the male dormitory to the female students. Anybody caught breaking this rule will be fined twenty dollars the first time."

He continued, "Anybody caught breaking this rule the second time will be fined sixty dollars. Being caught a third time will cost you a fine of one hundred eighty dollars. Are there any questions?"

A male student in the crowd inquired: "How much for a season pass?"

The following are actual excerpts from classified sections of city newspapers.

Illiterate? Write today for free help.

Stock up and save. Limit: one.

Semiannual after-Christmas sale.

Girl wanted to assist magician in cutting-off-head illusion. Blue Cross and salary.

Dinner special: Turkey $2.35; Chicken or Beef $2.25; Children $2.00.

Now is your chance to have your ears pierced and get an extra pair to take home too.

We do not tear your clothing with machinery. We do it carefully by hand.

Have several very old dresses from grandmother in beautiful condition.

Toaster: A gift that every member of the family appreciates. Automatically burns toast.

Christmas tag sale. Handmade gifts for the hard-to-find person.

Wanted: Man to take care of cow that does not smoke or drink.

And now, the superstore unequaled in size, unmatched in variety, unrivaled inconvenience.

A mafia family was in need of a collection officer; after screening many applicants, they hired an individual who happened to be deaf.

He was very good at what he did, and within a week he had collected $40,000 from nonpayers. However, he was greedy and hid the money for himself.

It didn't take long for the mafia bosses to catch on, so they sent a couple of thugs and an interpreter to find the collector. They found him, took him to an abandoned warehouse, and the two thugs told the interpreter to ask the collector, "Where's da money?"

The interpreter signed to the collector and the collector signed back, "I don't know what you're talking about."

The interpreter told them what he had said. One of the thugs pulled out a .38 revolver, stuck it in the collector's ear, and told the interpreter to ask him again.

"Where's da money?" the interpreter signed again.

The collector signed back, "It's in a tree stump in Central Park fifty yards east of the main fountain."

The interpreter told the thugs, "He said that he still doesn't know what you're talking about and that you don't have the guts to pull the trigger!"

An impecunious, starving artist was cornered by her landlord, who demanded that she pay him several months' back rent.

"Just think," the artist pleaded, "someday tourists will be pointing at that building and saying, 'The great abstract painter Celia Doggett used to live here.' "

"And if you don't pay up," the landlord countered, "they can come by tomorrow and say that."

What do you get when you cross an insomniac, an agnostic, and a dyslexic?

Someone who lies awake all night long wondering if there really is a Dog.

One day, a traveling salesman was driving down a back country road at about thirty miles an hour when he noticed that there was a three-legged chicken running along beside his car. He stepped on the gas, but at fifty miles per hour, the chicken was still keeping up.

After about a mile of running, the chicken ran up a farm lane and into a barn behind an old farmhouse.

The salesman had some time to kill, so he turned around and drove up the farm lane. He knocked at the door, and when the farmer answered, he told him what he had just seen.

The farmer said that he knew about the chicken. "As a matter of fact," the farmer said, "my son is a geneticist, and he developed this breed of chicken because the three of us each like a drumstick when we have chicken dinner, and this way we have to kill only one chicken."

The salesman said, "That's the most fantastic story I've ever heard. How do they taste?"

The farmer said, "I don't know. We can't catch 'em."

Things We Would Never Know Without the Movies

During all police investigations it will be necessary to visit a strip club at least once.

All telephone numbers in America begin with the digits 555.

Most dogs are immortal.

If being chased through town, you can usually take cover in a passing St. Patrick's Day parade—at any time of the year.

All beds have special L-shaped cover sheets that reach up to armpit-level on a woman but only to waist-level on the man lying beside her.

All grocery shopping bags contain at least one stick of French bread.

It's easy for anyone to land a plane, providing there is someone in the control tower to talk you down.

Once applied, lipstick will never rub off—even while scuba diving.

The ventilation system of any building is the perfect hiding place. No one will ever think of looking for you in there, and you can travel to any other part of the building you want without difficulty.

You're very likely to survive any battle in any war unless you make the mistake of showing someone a picture of your sweetheart back home.

Should you wish to pass yourself off as a German officer, it will not be necessary to speak the language. Even a bad German accent will do.

If your town is threatened by an imminent natural disaster or killer beast, the mayor's first concern will be the tourist trade or his forthcoming art exhibition.

The Eiffel Tower can be seen from any window in Paris.

A man will show no pain while taking the most ferocious beating but will wince uncontrollably when a woman tries to clean his wounds.

If a large pane of glass is visible, someone will be thrown through it before long.

When paying for a taxi, don't look at your wallet as you take out a bill. Just grab one at random and hand it over. It will always be the exact fare.

Kitchens don't have light switches. When entering a kitchen at night, you should open the fridge door and use that light instead.

If staying in a haunted house, women should investigate any strange noises in their most revealing underwear.

Word processors never display a cursor on-screen but will always say: Enter Password Now.

Mothers routinely cook eggs, bacon, and waffles for their family every morning even though their husband and children never have time to eat them.

Cars that crash will almost always burst into flames.

A single match will be sufficient to light up a room the size of a football stadium.

Medieval peasants had perfect teeth.

Although in the twentieth century it is possible to fire weapons at an object out of our visual range, people of the twenty-third century will have lost this technology.

Any person waking from a nightmare will sit bolt upright and pant.

It is not necessary to say hello or good-bye when beginning or ending phone conversations.

Even when driving down a perfectly straight road it is necessary to turn the steering wheel vigorously from left to right every few moments.

All bombs are fitted with electronic timing devices with large red readouts so you know exactly when they're going to go off.

It is always possible to park directly outside any building you are visiting.

A detective can solve a case only after he has been suspended from duty.

If you decide to start dancing in the street, everyone you bump into will know all the steps.

When a person is knocked unconscious by a blow to the head, he or she will never suffer a concussion or brain damage.

No one involved in a car chase, hijacking, explosion, volcanic eruption, or alien invasion will ever go into shock.

Police departments give their officers personality tests to make sure they are deliberately assigned a partner who is their total opposite.

When they are alone, all foreigners prefer to speak English to one another.

You can always find a chain saw when you need one.

Any lock can be picked in seconds by a credit card or a paper clip—unless it's the door to a burning building with a child trapped inside.

An electric fence, powerful enough to kill a dinosaur, will cause no lasting damage to an eight-year-old child.

Television news bulletins containing a story that affects you personally usually occur at that precise moment you turn the television on.

When the clothing store manager returned from lunch, he noticed his clerk's hand was bandaged, but before he could ask about the bandage, the clerk said he had some very good news for him.

"Guess what, sir?" the clerk said. "I finally sold that terrible, ugly suit we've had so long."

"Do you mean that repulsive pink-and-blue double-breasted thing?" the manager asked.

"That's the one."

"That's great!" the manager cried. "I thought we'd never get rid of that monstrosity. But tell me. Why is your hand bandaged?"

"Oh," the clerk replied, "after I sold the guy that suit, his guide dog bit me."

50 Actual Newspaper Headlines

(collected by actual journalists)

1. Something Went Wrong in Jet Crash, Expert Says
2. Police Begin Campaign to Run Down Jaywalkers
3. Safety Experts Say School Bus Passengers Should be Belted
4. Drunk Gets Nine Months in Violin Case
5. Survivor of Siamese Twins Joins Parents
6. Farmer Bill Dies in House
7. Iraqi Head Seeks Arms
8. Is There a Ring of Debris Around Uranus?
9. Stud Tires Out

10. Prostitutes Appeal to Pope
11. Panda Mating Fails; Veterinarian Takes Over
12. Soviet Virgin Lands Short of Goal Again
13. British Left Waffles on Falkland Islands
14. Lung Cancer in Women Mushrooms
15. Eye Drops Off Shelf
16. Teacher Strikes Idle Kids
17. Reagan Wins on Budget, But More Lies Ahead
18. Squad Helps Dog Bite Victim
19. Shot Off Woman's Leg Helps Nicklaus to 66
20. Enraged Cow Injures Farmer with Ax
21. Plane Too Close to Ground, Crash Probe Told
22. Miners Refuse to Work after Death
23. Juvenile Court to Try Shooting Defendant
24. Stolen Painting Found by Tree
25. Two Soviet Ships Collide, One Dies
26. Two Sisters Reunited after 18 Years in Checkout Counter
27. Killer Sentenced to Die for Second Time in 10 Years
28. Never Withhold Herpes Infection from Loved One
29. Drunken Drivers Paid $1,000 in '84
30. War Dims Hope for Peace

31. If Strike Isn't Settled Quickly, It May Last Awhile
32. Cold Wave Linked to Temperatures
33. Enfields Couple Slain; Police Suspect Homicide
34. Red Tape Holds Up New Bridge
35. Deer Kill 17,000
36. Typhoon Rips Through Cemetery; Hundreds Dead
37. Man Struck by Lightning Faces Battery Charge
38. New Study of Obesity Looks for Larger Test Group
39. Astronaut Takes Blame for Gas in Spacecraft
40. Kids Make Nutritious Snacks
41. Chef Throws His Heart into Helping Feed Needy
42. Arson Suspect Is Held in Massachusetts Fire
43. British Union Finds Dwarfs in Short Supply
44. Ban on Soliciting Dead in Trotwood
45. Lansing Residents Can Drop off Trees
46. Local High School Dropouts Cut in Half
47. New Vaccine May Contain Rabies
48. Man Minus Ear Waives Hearing
49. Deaf College Opens Doors to Hearing
50. Air Head Fired

Friends help you move. Real friends help you move bodies.

We are born naked, wet, and hungry. Then things get worse.

Suicidal twin kills sister by mistake!

Make it idiot proof, and someone will make a better idiot!

He who laughs last, thinks slowest!

Always remember you're unique, just like everybody else.

Lottery: a tax on people who are bad at math.

There's too much blood in my caffeine system.

Hard work has a future payoff. Laziness pays off now.

What is a "free" gift? Aren't all gifts free?

Puritanism: the haunting fear that someone, somewhere may be happy.

Consciousness: that annoying time between naps.

I used to have a handle on life, then it broke.

Don't take life too seriously, you'll never get out alive.

I don't suffer from insanity. I enjoy every minute of it.

Better to understand a little than to misunderstand a lot.

Where there's a will, I want to be in it.

Okay, who put a "stop payment" on my reality check?

Few women admit their age. Few men act theirs.

We have enough youth, how about a fountain of smart?

Change is inevitable, except from a vending machine.

The Pearly Gates

A guy died and was waiting at the Pearly Gates while St. Peter leafed through his big book to see if the guy was worthy. St. Peter went through the book several times, furrowed his brow, and said to the guy, "You know, I can't see that you ever did anything really bad in your life, but you never did anything really good, either. If you can point to even one *really* good deed, you're in."

The fellow thought for a moment, and said, "Yeah, there was one time when I was driving down the highway and saw a giant group of bikers assaulting this poor girl. I slowed down my car to see what was going on, and, sure enough, there they were, about fifty of them, tormenting this terrified young woman. Infuriated, I got out of my car, grabbed a tire iron out of my trunk, and walked up to the leader of the gang, a huge guy with a studded leather jacket and a chain running from his nose to his ear. As I walked up to the leader, the bikers formed a circle around me. So I ripped the leader's chain off his face and smashed him over the head with the tire iron. Laid him out. Then I turned and yelled at the rest of them, 'Leave this poor innocent girl alone! You're all a bunch of sick, deranged animals! Go home before I teach you all a lesson in pain!' "

St. Peter, impressed, says, "Really? When did this happen?"

"Oh, about two minutes ago."

Three guys were met at the Pearly Gates by St. Peter. He told them, "I know that you guys are forgiven because you're here. Before I let you into heaven, I have to ask you something. Your answer will depend on what kind of car you get. You have to have a car in heaven because heaven is so big." Peter asked the first guy, "How long were you married?"

The first guy replied, "Twenty-four years."

"Did you ever cheat on your wife?" Peter asked.

The guy said, "Yeah, seven times . . . but you said I was forgiven."

Peter said, "Yeah, but that's not too good. Here's a Pinto for you to drive."

The second guy got the same question from Peter. He replied, "I was married for forty-one years and cheated on her once, but that was our first year and we really worked it out well."

Peter said, "I'm pleased to hear that, here's a Lincoln for you."

The third guy walked up and said, "Peter, I know what you're going to ask. I was married for sixty-three years and didn't even look at another woman. I treated my wife like a queen!"

Peter said, "That's what I like to hear. Here's a Jaguar for you."

A little while later, the two guys with the Pinto and the Lincoln saw the guy with the Jaguar crying on the golden sidewalk. They went over to see what was the matter. When they asked the guy with the Jaguar what was wrong, he said, "I just saw my wife. She was on a skateboard!"

Three blondes died and were up being interviewed by St. Peter. He said, "I have one question, and if you answer correctly, I will let you into heaven." He asked the first blonde, "What is Easter?"

She answered, "Oh, that's that one time of the year when our whole family gets together and we eat turkey."

St. Peter just shook his head and said to the next blonde, "What is Easter?"

She replied, "Oh, that is the time of year when our family gets together and we all open presents and the fat, jolly guy comes down the chimney."

Again St. Peter just shook his head. He asked the third blonde, "What is Easter?"

She said, "Oh, that's when Christ died and they put him in a tomb and rolled a rock in front of it."

St. Peter smiled and urged her, "Yes, go on. . . ."

The blonde continued, "Then once a year we roll the

stone away and he comes out, and if he sees his shadow, we have six more weeks of winter."

In a small country pub, all the patrons became quite used to the pub owners' little dog being around the bar, so they were quite upset when one day the little dog died.

Everyone met to decide how they could remember the little dog. The decision was to cut off his tail and stick it up behind the bar to remind everyone of the little dog's wagging tail.

The little dog went up to heaven and was about to run through the Pearly Gates when he was stopped by St. Peter, who questioned the little dog as to where he was going.

The little dog said, "I have been a good dog, so I am going into heaven where I belong!"

St. Peter replied, "Heaven is a place of perfection; you cannot come into heaven without a tail. Where is your tail?"

The little dog explained what had happened back on Earth.

St. Peter told the little dog to go back down to Earth and retrieve his tail. The little dog protested that it was now the middle of the night on Earth, but St. Peter would not change his mind.

So the little dog went back down to Earth and scratched on the door of the pub until the bartender who lived upstairs came down and opened the door. "My goodness, it is the spirit of the little dog. What can I do for you?" said the bartender.

The little dog explained that he wasn't allowed into heaven without his tail, and he needed it back.

The bartender replied, "I would really like to help you, but my liquor license doesn't allow me to retail spirits after hours!"

There once was an consultant who lived her whole life without ever taking advantage of any of the people she worked for. In fact, she made sure that every job she did resulted in a win-win situation.

One day while walking down the street, she was tragically killed when she was struck by a bus.

Her soul arrived up in heaven, where she was met at the Pearly Gates by St. Peter himself. "Welcome to heaven," said St. Peter. "Before you get settled in, though, it seems we have a problem. You see, strangely enough, we've never once had a consultant make it this far, and we're not really sure what to do with you."

"No problem, just let me in," said the consultant.

"Well, I'd like to, but I have higher orders. What we're going to do is let you have a day in hell and a day in heaven and then you can choose which place you want to spend an eternity in."

"Actually, I think I've made up my mind. . . . I'd prefer to stay in heaven."

"Sorry, we do have rules. . . ." And with that, St. Peter put the consultant in an elevator, and it went down to hell. The doors opened and the consultant found herself stepping out onto the putting green of a beautiful golf course. In the distance was a country club, and standing in front of her were all her friends—fellow consultants with whom she had worked, all dressed in evening gowns and cheering for her. They ran up and kissed her on both cheeks, and they talked about old times. They played an excellent round of golf, and at night they went to the country club, where she enjoyed an excellent steak and lobster dinner.

She met the devil, who was actually a really nice guy, and she had a great time telling jokes and dancing. The consultant was having such a good time that before she knew it, it was time to leave. Everybody shook her hand and waved good-bye as she got on the elevator.

The elevator went up and opened back up at the Pearly Gates, where St. Peter was waiting for her.

"Now it's time to spend a day in heaven."

So the consultant spent the next twenty-four hours lounging around on the clouds and playing the harp and singing. She had a great time, and before she knew it her twenty-four hours were up and St. Peter came and got her.

"So, you've spent a day in hell and you've spent a day in heaven. Now you must choose your place of eternal dwelling."

The consultant paused for a second and then replied, "Well, I never thought I'd say this—I mean, heaven has been really great and all—but I think I had a better time in hell."

So St. Peter escorted her to the elevator, and again the consultant went down to hell.

When the doors of the elevator opened, she found herself standing in a desolate wasteland covered in garbage and filth. She saw her friends now dressed in rags, picking up the garbage and putting it in sacks.

The devil came up to her and put his arm around her.

"I don't understand," stammered the consultant. "Yesterday I was here and there was a golf course and a country club and we ate lobster and we danced and had a great time. Now all there is is a wasteland of garbage, and all my friends look miserable."

The devil looked at her and smiled. "That's because yesterday we were recruiting you, but today you're staff."

Two men waiting at the Pearly Gates strike up a conversation.

"How'd you die?" the first man asks the second.

"I froze to death," says the second.

"That's awful," says the first man. "How does it feel to freeze to death?"

"It's very uncomfortable at first," says the second man. "You get the shakes, and you get pains in all your fingers and toes. But eventually, it's a very calm way to go. You get numb and you kind of drift off, as if you're sleeping. How about you, how did you die?"

"I had a heart attack," says the first man. "You see, I knew my wife was cheating on me, so one day I showed up at home unexpectedly. I ran up to the bedroom and found her alone, knitting. I ran down to the basement, but no one was hiding there. I ran up to the second floor, but no one was hiding there, either. I ran as fast as I could to the attic, and just as I got there, I had a massive heart attack and died."

The second man shakes his head. "That's so ironic," he says.

"What do you mean?" asks the first man.

"If you had only stopped to look in the freezer, we'd both still be alive."

An eighty-five-year-old couple, married for almost sixty years, died in a car crash. They had been in good health the last ten years, mainly as a result of her interest in health food and exercise.

When they reached the Pearly Gates, St. Peter took them to their mansion, which was decked out with a beautiful kitchen and a master bath suite with a sauna and Jacuzzi. As they "oohed and aahed" the old man asked Peter how much all this was going to cost.

"It's free," Peter replied. "This is heaven."

Next they went out back to survey the championship golf course that the home backed up to. They would have golfing privileges every day, and each week the course would change to a new one that represented one of the great golf courses on Earth. The old man asked, "What are the green fees?"

Peter's reply: "This is heaven; you play for free."

Next they went to the clubhouse and saw the lavish buffet lunch with the cuisines of the world laid out. "How much to eat?" asked the old man.

"Don't you understand yet? This is heaven; it is free!" Peter replied with some exasperation.

"Well, where are the low-fat and low-cholesterol tables?" the old man asked timidly.

Peter lectured, "That's the best part: You can eat as much as you like of whatever you like and you never get fat and you never get sick. This is heaven."

With that, the old man threw down his hat, stomped on it, and shrieked wildly.

Peter and his wife both tried to calm him down, asking him what was wrong.

The old man looked at his wife and said, "This is all your fault. If it weren't for your blasted bran muffins, I could have been here ten years ago!"

A guy's in his house when horrendous rains come up. The water starts rising, and before you know it, a major flood is under way. Roads are rivers. Nothing's moving.

Pretty soon, a boat comes along. A man in the boat yells to the guy in the house, "Come on—we're here to save you. Get in the boat."

They guy in the house says, "No . . . I've got faith that God will save me."

The boat leaves.

The water keeps rising. The guy is forced up to the second floor of his house by the floodwaters.

Another boat comes along. A man in the boat yells, "Come on! It's getting worse. If you don't get in the boat, you're going to drown!"

From the second-floor window, the guy says, "No . . . I'll be okay. I've got faith in God that he'll save me."

The boat leaves. Water's rising. The guy's on the roof.

A helicopter hovers overhead and the pilot shouts out, "This is your last chance. Climb up the ladder. If you don't come now, you're going to drown."

The guy says from the roof, "No, thanks. God will save me."

The pilot shrugs his shoulders and splits.

The water rises. The guy drowns. At the Pearly Gates, he asks St. Peter, "What happened? I've been devoted to God and had absolute faith that he would save me. Why did he let me down?"

And St. Peter tells him, "What the heck do you want? God sent you two boats and a helicopter!"

A lawyer died and arrived at the Pearly Gates. To his dismay, there were thousands of people ahead of him in line to see St. Peter.

To his surprise, St. Peter left his desk at the gate and came down the long line to where the lawyer was and greeted him warmly. Then St. Peter and one of his assistants took the lawyer by the hands and guided him up to the front of the line and into a comfortable chair by his desk.

The lawyer said, "I don't mind all this attention, but what makes me so special?"

St. Peter replied, "Well, I've added up all the hours for which you billed your clients, and by my calculation you must be about a hundred and ninety-three years old!"

There were three men standing at the Pearly Gates. St. Peter came out to meet them and asked, "What would each of you like to hear your relatives or friends say at your funeral?"

The first man answered, "I am a renowned doctor,

and I would love to hear someone say how I had been instrumental in saving people's lives and giving them a second chance."

The second man replied, "I am a family man and a schoolteacher. I would like to hear some say what a great husband and father I was and that I had made a difference in some young person's life."

The third man replied, "Wow, guys, those are really great things, but I guess if I had my choice I would rather hear someone say, " 'Look! He's moving!' "

Pets and Other Animals

A man came home from work one day to find his dog with his neighbor's pet rabbit in his mouth. The rabbit was dead, and the guy panicked. He was sure the neighbors would demand that his dog be destroyed. So he took the dirty, chewed-up rabbit into the house, gave it a bath, blow-dried its fur, and put it back into the cage in the neighbor's garage, hoping they would think it died of natural causes.

A few days later, his neighbor called across the hedge to the guy: "Did you hear that Fluffy died?"

The guy stammered around a bit and said, "Um . . . no . . . um . . . what happened?"

The neighbor replied, "We just found him dead in his cage one day. But the weird thing is that the day after we buried him, we went out into the garage and someone had dug him up, given him a bath, and put him back into the cage. There are some real sick people out there!"

A guy with a Doberman Pinscher said to a guy with a Chihuahua, "Let's go over to that restaurant and get something to eat."

The guy with the Chihuahua replied, "We can't go in there. We've got dogs with us."

The guy with the Doberman Pinscher said, "Just follow my lead."

They walked over to the restaurant, and the guy with the Doberman Pinscher put on a pair of dark glasses. He walked into the restaurant.

The host at the door said, "Sorry, no pets allowed. State law."

The guy with the Doberman Pinscher said, "You don't understand. This is my Seeing Eye dog."

The host was stymied. "A Doberman Pinscher?"

"Yes, they're using them now; they're very good."

The host shrugged and said, "Come on in."

The guy with the Chihuahua figured, "What the heck," so he put on a pair of dark glasses and started to walk in.

The host said, "Sorry, pal, no pets allowed."

The guy with the Chihuahua said, "You don't understand. This is my Seeing Eye dog."

The host said, "Oh, come on, a Chihuahua?"

The guy with the Chihuahua said, "You mean they gave me a Chihuahua?"

Recently the director of a local municipal zoo, having acquired a rare Indonesian ape named Oscar, was quite displeased to find that the large, aggressive animal had broken free from his cage and was roaming throughout the city. The matter was serious because the members of the staff of the zoo, while expert at caring for animals, had had no experience in capturing them.

The zoo director appealed to the office of the mayor for help, and the secretary to the mayor asked, "Have you looked in the Yellow Pages?"

The director said he hadn't, but would do so immediately. To his surprise, under "Animal Capturing Service," he found a listing for the A-1 Ape Apprehenders. He called them and within twenty minutes a truck arrived at the administration office of the zoo.

A small man emerged and rushed to the director, who was waiting at the door.

"Is there a wooded area in the vicinity?" the little man asked.

The director said there was, about a half mile away.

"Hop in the truck," the little man said.

The director did, and they drove off. Minutes later they arrived at a small grove and immediately spotted Oscar on a tree branch about twenty-five feet above the ground.

The two men got out, went to the back of the truck, and the little man opened the door. An excited little dog jumped out and began running around in circles.

The little man reached into the truck and took out a suitcase, which he opened. In the suitcase were a pair of handcuffs, which he handed to the zoo director, a sawed-off shotgun, which he leaned against the trunk of the tree, and a baseball bat.

"Now," the little man said, "I'm going up into the tree with the baseball bat, and I'm going to knock the ape out of the tree. The instant the ape hits the ground the dog will grab at his crotch. The ape, instantly and instinctively, will grab his crotch with both hands. You snap the handcuffs on and we've got him."

The zoo director, pointing to the shotgun leaning against the tree, said, "I'm not too sure about this. What's the gun for?"

The little man said, "Look, I'm an expert. I know what I'm doing, and things will go just fine. After all, I have the baseball bat. I know my job and it'll never happen, but if the ape should, by any chance, knock *me* out of the tree, *shoot the dog*!"

A poor little lonely old lady lived in a house with only her cat as a friend. One day, the lights went out as she sat knitting; she had been unable to pay the electric bill. So she went up to the attic and got an old oil lamp from her childhood. As she rubbed it clean a genie appeared and allowed her three wishes.

"First, I want to be so rich I never have to worry about money again.

"Second, I want to be young and beautiful again.

"And last, I want you to change my little cat into a handsome prince."

There was a mild explosion and a huge blue puff of smoke filled the attic.

As the smoke cleared she saw she was surrounded by big bags of coins, and that in the mirror she saw a beautiful young woman.

She turned as the handsome prince walked in the

door, held her in his arms, and said, "Now I'll bet you're sorry you took me to the vet for that little operation."

What do you get when you run over a parakeet with a lawn mower?

Shredded tweet.

Bob received a parrot for his birthday. The parrot was fully grown, with a bad attitude and worse vocabulary. Every other word was an expletive. Those that weren't expletives were, to say the least, rude. Bob tried hard to change the bird's attitude and was constantly saying polite words, playing soft music, doing anything he could think of to try to set a good example.

Nothing worked. He yelled at the bird, and the bird got worse. He shook the bird, and the bird became angrier and ruder. Finally, in a moment of desperation, Bob put the parrot in the freezer. For a few moments he heard the bird squawking and cursing—and then suddenly there was quiet.

Bob was afraid he had actually hurt the bird and quickly opened the freezer door.

The parrot calmly stepped out onto Bob's extended arm and said: "I'm sorry that I might have offended you with my language and actions and ask for your forgiveness. I will endeavor to correct my behavior."

Bob was astonished at the bird's change in attitude and was about to ask what had made such a drastic change when the parrot said: "Sir, may I ask what the chicken did?"

A Jehovah's Witness knocked on the front door of a home, and heard a faint, high-pitched, "Come in."

He tried the door, and it was locked, so he went around to the back door. He knocked again and heard again the high-pitched, "Come in."

As he entered the kitchen a large, mean, snarling Doberman met him. As he plastered himself against the wall, he called out for help.

Again, he heard, "Come in."

Sliding against the wall, he entered the living room and saw a parrot in cage. He said, "For Pete's sake, is 'Come in' all you can say?"

The parrot laughed and said, "Sic 'im."

A guy walks into a bar with a dog under his arm, puts the dog on the bar, and announces that the dog can talk and that he has $100 he's willing to bet anyone who says he can't. The bartender quickly takes the bet, and the owner looks at the dog and asks, "What's the thing on top of this building that keeps the rain from coming inside?"

The dog answers, "ROOF." The bartender says, "Who are you kidding? I'm not paying."

The dogs owner says, "How about double or nothing and I'll ask him something else?" The bartender agrees and the owner turns to the dog and asks, "Who was the greatest ballplayer of all time?"

The dog answers with a muffled "RUTH." With that the bartender picks them both up and tosses them out the door.

As they bounce on the sidewalk the dog looks at his owner and says, "DiMaggio?"

A farmer with lots of chickens posted the following sign: FREE CHICKENS. OUR COOP RUNNETH OVER.

A local business was looking for office help. They put a sign in the window, stating the following: "HELP WANTED. Must be able to type, must be good with a computer, and must be bilingual. We are an Equal Opportunity Employer."

A short time afterward, a dog trotted up to the window, saw the sign, and went inside. He looked at the receptionist and wagged his tail, then walked over to the sign, looked at it, and whined.

Getting the idea, the receptionist got the office manager. The office manager looked at the dog and was surprised, to say the least. However, the dog looked determined, so the office manager led him into the office. Inside, the dog jumped up on the chair and stared at the manager.

The manager said, "I can't hire you. The sign says you have to be able to type."

The dog jumped down, went to the typewriter, and proceeded to type out a perfect letter. He took out the page, trotted over to the manager, and gave it to him, then jumped back on the chair.

The manager was stunned, but then told the dog, "The sign says you have to be good with a computer."

The dog jumped down again and went to the computer. He proceeded to enter and execute a perfect program that worked flawlessly the first time.

By this time the manager was totally dumbfounded! He looked at the dog and said, "I realize that you are a very intelligent dog and have some interesting abilities. However, I *still* can't give you the job."

The dog jumped down and went to a copy of the sign and put his paw on the sentence that proclaimed the company an Equal Opportunity Employer.

The manager said, "Yes, but the sign *also* says that you have to be bilingual."

The dog looked at the manager calmly and said, "Meow."

An elderly woman woke up one morning and found her sixteen-year-old dog lying on the floor. "Oh, no," she said, "there must be something wrong with Scruffy!"

She scooped up the dog and rushed him to the vet. "Doctor, please help," she implored as she put him on the table.

After a brief examination, the doctor said, "I'm sorry, madam, but I believe your dog has died."

"Oh, but there must be something you can do," said the woman.

"Well, there is one thing," said the vet as he pulled

a sack from the nearby closet. The vet opened the sack and placed a scrawny old cat on the table next to the dog. The cat looked at the dog and hissed. It circled the dog cautiously, sniffing and hissing.

The vet put the cat back in the bag and told the woman, "There is nothing more I can do."

The old woman said, "I guess you're right, Doctor. Scruffy hates cats, and if he weren't dead he surely would have barked."

The vet said that he would take care of the arrangements for Scruffy, and the old woman went home.

Three weeks later, the old woman received a bill from the vet for $338. The old woman thought there must be a mistake, so she called the vet for an explanation. The vet pulled out the bill and told the woman that he had charged her $38 for taking care of Scruffy's arrangements.

The old woman said, "That seems fair, but I don't understand what the $300 is for."

"Oh," said the vet, "that was for the cat scan."

A burglar breaks into a house in the best area of town. He's sure that there's nobody home, but he sneaks in, doesn't turn on any lights, and heads for where he thinks the valuables are kept. Then he hears a voice say, "I can see you! Jesus can see you too!"

He freezes in his tracks. He doesn't move a muscle. A couple of minutes go by. The voice repeats, "I can see you! Jesus can see you too!"

He slowly takes out his flashlight, switches it on, and looks around the room. He sees a birdcage with a parrot in it. "Did you say that?" he asks the parrot.

The parrot says again, "I can see you! Jesus can see you too!"

"Hah! So what? You're just a parrot," says the burglar.

"I may be just a parrot," replies the parrot. "But Jesus is a Doberman!"

Four men were bragging about their smart dogs. The first man was an engineer, the second was an accountant, the third was a chemist, and the fourth man was a government worker.

To show off, the engineer called to his dog, "T-Square, do your stuff." T-Square trotted over to a desk, took out some paper and a pen, and promptly drew a circle, a square, and a triangle. Everyone agreed that was pretty smart.

But the accountant said his dog could do better. He said, "Slide Rule, do your stuff." Slide Rule went out into the kitchen and returned with a dozen cookies. He divided them into four equal piles of three cookies each. Everyone agreed that was good.

The chemist said his dog could do better still, so he called his dog and said, "Measure, do your stuff." Measure got up, walked over to the fridge, took out a quart of milk, got a ten-ounce glass from the cupboard and poured exactly eight ounces without spilling a drop. Everyone agreed that was great.

The government worker called to his dog and said, "Coffee Break, do your stuff!" Coffee Break jumped to his feet, ate the cookies, drank the milk, dumped on the paper, sexually assaulted the other three dogs, claimed he injured his back while doing so, filed a grievance for unsafe working conditions, put in for Worker's Compensation, and went home on sick leave.

•

A woman goes into a store and buys a beautiful green and blue parrot. But the only words the parrot knows how to say are "Who is it?"

She takes the parrot home but soon realizes that the bird's colors clash horribly with the living room. So she calls an interior designer, who says he will come by shortly. When the decorator comes, the woman is out shopping. He knocks on the door, and the parrot says, "Who is it?"

The man says, "It's the decorator."

The parrot says, "Who is it?"

The man says, "It's the decorator."

The parrot says, "Who is it?"

The man says, "It's the decorator!"

The parrot says, "Who is it?"

The man screams, "The decorator!"

The decorator gets so mad that he has a stroke and dies on the spot.

The lady comes home and finds the dead man lying on her front porch. She says, "Oh, my gosh! Who is it?"

The parrot replies, "It's the decorator!"

Two hikers were walking through central Pennsylvania when they came upon a six-foot-wide hole in the ground. They figured it must be the opening for a vertical air shaft from an old abandoned coal mine. Curious about the depth of the hole, the first hiker picked up a nearby rock and tossed it into the opening. They listened . . . and heard nothing.

The second hiker picked up an even larger rock and tossed it into the opening.

They listened . . . and still heard nothing. Then they both picked up an old railroad tie, dragged it to the edge of the shaft, and hurled it down. Seconds later a dog came running up between the two men and jumped straight into the hole. Bewildered, the two men just looked at each other, trying to figure out why a dog would do such a thing.

Soon a young boy ambled onto the scene and asked if either man had seen a dog around here. The hikers told him about the dog that had just jumped into the hole.

The young boy laughed and said, "That couldn't be my dog. My dog was tied to a railroad tie!"

A veterinarian and a taxidermist went into business together. Their slogan: "Either way, you get your pet back."

Politics

Clinton, Dole, and Perot were on a long flight on Air Force One. Perot pulled out a $100 bill and said, "I'm going to throw this hundred-dollar bill out and make someone down below happy."

Dole, not wanting to be outdone, said, "If that were my hundred-dollar bill, I would split it into two fifties and make two people down below happy."

Of course, Clinton didn't want these two candidates to outdo him either, so he piped in, "I would instead take a hundred one-dollar bills and throw them out to make a hundred people just a little happier."

At that point the pilot, who had overheard all this bragging and couldn't stand it anymore, came out of the cockpit and said, "I think I'll throw all three of you out of this plane and make two hundred fifty million people happy."

What's the difference between the government and the Mafia?

One of them is organized.

Dan Quayle, Bob Dole, and Bill Clinton were traveling in a car together in the Midwest. A tornado came along, whirled them up into the air, and tossed them thousands of yards away. When they came to and extracted themselves from the vehicle, they realized they were in the Land of Oz. They decided to go see the Wizard of Oz.

Quayle said, "I'm going to ask the Wizard for a brain."

Dole said, "I'm going to ask the Wizard for a heart."

Clinton said, "Where's Dorothy?"

You Might Be a Republican If . . .

You've tried to argue that poverty could be abolished if people were allowed to keep more of their minimum wage.

You're a pro-lifer but support the death penalty.

You've ever uttered the phrase, "Why don't we just bomb the sons of bitches?"

You've ever called a secretary or waitress "Honey."

You don't let your kids watch *Sesame Street* because you accuse Bert and Ernie of "sexual deviance."

You use any of these terms to describe your wife: "old ball and chain," "little woman," and/or "tax credit."

You think Birkenstock was that radical rock concert in 1969.

Vietnam makes a lot of sense to you.

You've ever said, "Clean air? Looks clean to me."

You've ever called education a luxury.

You wonder if donations to the Pentagon are tax-deductible.

You've ever based an argument on the phrase, "Well, tradition dictates . . ."

You think all artists are gay.

You ever told a child that Oscar the Grouch "lives in a trash can because he is lazy and doesn't want to contribute to society."

You've ever urged someone to pull themselves up by their bootstraps, when they don't even have shoes.

You Might be a Democrat If . . .

You think the rich can get richer off people who have no money.

You've named your kids "Stardust" or "Moonbeam."

You've uttered the phrase "There ought to be a law" at least once a week.

You have ever found yourself nodding vigorously and saying, "Someone finally said it right" during an episode of *Oprah.*

All of your 1970s BEWARE OF GLOBAL FREEZING signs now have BEWARE OF GLOBAL WARMING on the back.

Your friends told you how much fun you had at the Grateful Dead show, but you're not sure what year you saw them.

You know more than two people who have a degree in "Womyn's Studies."

You blame things on "The Man."

You have ever argued that the only flaw with Marx is that Russia was an agrarian society.

You've ever called the meter maid a fascist.

You are giddy at the prospect of the return of bell bottoms.

You view Jane Fonda as a courageous heroine with strong convictions.

After looking at your pay stub you can still say, "America is undertaxed."

You know two or more people with "concrete proof" that the Pentagon is covering up Roswell, the Kennedy assassination, or the CIA's role in creating AIDS.

You came of age in the 1960s and don't remember.

You've ever owned a VW bug or ridden in a Microbus.

You own something that says *Dukakis for President* and still display it.

You've ever argued that with just one more year of

welfare that person will turn it around and get off drugs.

You keep count of how many people you know in each racial or ethnic category.

You believe that a few hundred loggers can find another career, but the defenseless spotted owl must live in its preferred tree.

You've tried to argue in favor of anything based on, "Well, they're gonna do it anyway, so . . ."

You paid $5,000 for a beer keg once used by John F. Kennedy.

You protested American intervention in Vietnam but support American intervention in Haiti, Somolia, and Bosnia.

You ever drove to an Earth Day rally in a Lincoln Towncar.

You object to little old ladies wearing fur but not big, mean bikers wearing leather.

You own an espresso maker, a Cuisinart, a microwave oven, and a heated water bed and yet oppose offshore oil drilling and the construction of nuclear power plants.

You are against prayer in public schools, even before math tests.

A Republican, a Libertarian, and a Democrat are seated separately in a restaurant when a poor man walks in; unbeknownst to any of them, it is Jesus.

The Republican summons the waiter and asks him to serve the poor man the best food in the house and put it on his tab; the waiter does so.

The Libertarian asks the waiter to please serve the poor man iced tea and to put it on his tab. The waiter does so.

The Democrat then asks the waiter to bring the poor man pecan pie with ice cream and to put it on his tab.

When Jesus is finished eating, he goes over to the Republican and says, "I was hungry, and you gave me something to eat. Thank you. I see you are blind." He touches the man's eye, and his blindness is healed.

Jesus then goes over to the Libertarian and says, "I was thirsty, and you gave me something to drink. Thank you. I see you have a bad arm." He touches the man's arm, and it is healed.

Then Jesus walks over to the Democrat. The Democrat moves away from Jesus and exclaims, "Don't touch me! I'm on a hundred percent disability!"

During a terrible snowstorm, all the highway signs were covered with snow. The following spring, the state decided to raise all the signs twelve inches at a cost of six million dollars.

"That's an outrageous price!" said a local farmer, "but I guess we're lucky the state handled it instead of the federal government."

"Why's that?"

"Because knowing the federal government, they'd decide to lower all the highways."

FEUDALISM: You have two cows. Your lord takes some of the milk.

PURE SOCIALISM: You have two cows. The government takes them and puts them in a barn with everyone else's cows. You have to take care of all the cows. The government gives you as much milk as you need.

BUREAUCRATIC SOCIALISM: You have two cows. The government takes them and puts them in a barn with everyone else's cows. They are cared for by ex-chicken farmers. You have to take care of the chickens the government took from the chicken farmers. The government gives you as much milk and as many eggs as the regulations say you should need.

FASCISM: You have two cows. The government takes both, hires you to take care of them, and sells you the milk.

PURE COMMUNISM: You have two cows. Your neighbors help you take care of them, and you all share the milk.

RUSSIAN COMMUNISM: You have two cows. You have to take care of them, but the government takes all the milk.

DICTATORSHIP: You have two cows. The government takes both and shoots you.

SINGAPOREAN DEMOCRACY: You have two cows. The government fines you for keeping two unlicensed farm animals in an apartment.

MILITARIANISM: You have two cows. The government takes both and drafts you.

PURE DEMOCRACY: You have two cows. Your neighbors decide who gets the milk.

REPRESENTATIVE DEMOCRACY: You have two cows. Your neighbors pick someone to tell you who gets the milk.

AMERICAN DEMOCRACY: The government promises to give you two cows if you vote for it. After the election, the president is impeached for speculating in cow futures. The press dubs the affair "Cowgate."

BRITISH DEMOCRACY: You have two cows. You feed them sheep's brains and they go mad. The government doesn't do anything.

BUREAUCRACY: You have two cows. At first the government regulates what you can feed them and when you can milk them. Then it pays you not to milk them. After that it takes both, shoots one, milks the other, and pours the milk down the drain. Then it requires you to fill out forms accounting for the missing cow.

ANARCHY: You have two cows. Either you sell the milk at a fair price or your neighbors try to kill you and take the cows.

CAPITALISM: You have two cows. You sell one and buy a bull.

HONG KONG CAPITALISM: You have two cows. You sell three of them to your publicly listed company, using letters of credit opened by your brother-in-law at the bank, then execute a debt/equity swap with associated general offer so that you get all four cows back, with a tax deduction for keeping five cows. The milk rights of six cows are transferred via a Panamanian intermediary to a Cayman Islands company secretly owned by the majority shareholder, who sells the rights to all seven cows' milk back to the listed company. The annual report says that the company owns eight cows, with an option on one more. Meanwhile, you kill the two cows because the feng shui is bad.

ENVIRONMENTALISM: You have two cows. The government forbids you to milk or kill them.

TOTALITARIANISM: You have two cows. The government takes them and denies they ever existed. Milk is banned.

SURREALISM: You have two giraffes. The government requires you to take harmonica lessons.

LIBERTARIANISM: You have two cows. One has actually read the Constitution, believes in it, and has some really good ideas about government. The cow runs for office, and while most people agree that the cow is the best candidate, nobody except the other cow votes for her because they think it would be "throwing their vote away."

G. Gordon Liddy, Oliver North, and Ted Kennedy are captured by the enemy and sentenced to fifty lashes for spying. The colonel was in a kindly mood and allowed them a choice of something to put on their backs.

"What do you want on your back, Liddy?" the colonel barked.

"Nuthin'," huffed Liddy. He received his lashes without a sound.

"What do you want on your back, North?"

"Suntan oil, please," answered North. As the whip descended time after time, North screamed in pain.

"What do you want on your back, Teddy?" the colonel asked for the third time.

"Liddy," answered Kennedy.

Rednecks and City Slickers

A city slicker moves to the country and decides he's going to take up farming. He heads to the local co-op and tells the man, "Give me a hundred baby chickens." The co-op man complies.

A week later the man returns and says, "Give me two hundred baby chickens." The co-op man complies.

Again, a week later the man returns. This time he says, "Give me five hundred baby chickens."

"Wow!" the co-op man replies. "You must really be doing well!"

"Naw," said the man with a sigh. "I'm either planting them too deep or too far apart!"

Actual Titles of Country Songs

1. Her Teeth Was Stained, But Her Heart Was Pure
2. How Can I Miss You, If You Won't Go Away?
3. Get Your Biscuits in the Oven, And Your Buns in Bed
4. Get Your Tongue Outta My Mouth, 'Cause I'm Kissing You Good-bye
5. I Can't Get Over You, So Why Don't You Get Under Me?
6. I Don't Know Whether to Kill Myself, or Go Bowling
7. She Got the Ring and I Got the Finger
8. You're the Reason Our Kids Are So Ugly
9. I Just Bought a Car from a Guy That Stole My Girl, but the Car Don't Run, So I Figure We Got an Even Deal
10. I Keep Forgettin' I Forgot About You
11. I Liked You Better, Before I Knew You So Well
12. I Still Miss You Baby, But My Aim's Gettin' Better
13. I Wouldn't Take Her to a Dog Fight, 'Cause I'm Afraid She'd Win
14. I'll Marry You Tomorrow, But Let's Honeymoon Tonite
15. I'm So Miserable Without You, It's Like Having You Here

16. Please Bypass This Heart?
17. If I Had Shot You When I Wanted to, I'd Be Out by Now
18. Mama Get a Hammer (There's a Fly on Papa's Head)
19. My Head Hurts, My Feet Stink, and I Don't Love Jesus
20. My Wife Ran off with My Best Friend, and I Sure Do Miss Him
21. You've Done Something to My Heart That I Can't Fix with Duct Tape

A redneck and a city slicker were on death row in an Alabama prison. When their very last appeals were turned down by the governor, the prison warden came to them with the bad news.

"Well, boys, it's time for you to die. You're each allowed a final request."

The two men thought for a moment; then the redneck said, "Warden, for my last request, I'd like to hear 'Achy-Breaky Heart' just one more time."

The warden cringed, then nodded his assent. "Okay," he said. "Now what about you? What's your last request?" he asked the city slicker.

"Warden," asked the city slicker, "can I go first?"

Two young rednecks were camping out in the forest one night. But the mosquitoes were so fierce that the boys had to hide under their blankets to keep from getting bitten.

Then one of the boys saw some lightning bugs. "We may as well give up," he told his friend. "Now they're coming at us with flashlights."

Two rednecks were driving down the highway, drinking beer, when flashing lights from a policeman appeared in the driver's rearview mirror.

"Don't worry!" says the driver to his friend. "Just do exactly what I tell you and everything will work out fine. First, we'll peel the labels off our beer bottles and we'll each stick one on our forehead. Now shove all of the bottles under the front seat! And let me do all the talking!"

They pulled over to the side of the road and the cop walked up to the car. He shined his flashlight into the car and looked at the two drunks.

"Have you been drinking?" he asked them.

"Oh, no, sir," replied the driver.

"I noticed you weaving back and forth across the highway. Are you sure you haven't been drinking?" the cop asked.

"Oh, no, sir," the driver answered. "We haven't had a thing to drink tonight."

"Well, I've got to ask you," said the cop, "What on earth are those things on your forehead?"

"That's easy, Officer," said the driver. "You see, we're both alcoholics, and we're on the patch!"

Billy Joe frantically called the hospital. "My wife's going into labor—you gotta send help!" he cried.

"Relax now," the nurse said calmly. "Is this her first child?"

"No!" Billy Joe replied. "This is her husband!"

Why don't rednecks ever call 911 in an emergency?

They can't find "eleven" on the phone dial.

A hillbilly family took a vacation to New York City.

One day, the father took his son into a large building. They were amazed by everything they saw, especially the elevator at one end of the lobby.

The boy asked, "What's this, Paw?"

The father responded, "Son, I have never seen anything like this in my life. I don't know what it is!"

While the boy and his father were watching in wide-eyed astonishment, an old lady in a wheelchair rolled up to the moving walls and pressed a button. The walls opened and the lady rolled between them into a small room. The walls closed and the boy and his father watched small circles of lights above the walls light up. They continued to watch the circles light up in the reverse direction. The walls opened again, and a voluptuous twenty-four-year-old woman stepped out.

The father turned to his son and said, "Go get your maw."

A pickup truck with two rednecks in it pulled into a lumberyard. Jethro tumbled out and went into the office. "I need some four-by-twos," he announced.

"You must mean two-by-fours," the yard manager replied.

Jethro scratched his head. "Wait a minute, I'll go check," he said.

He returned to the truck and had a long conversation with C.W. Then he returned to the office. "Yeah," he said, "I mean two-by-fours."

"Okay," said the manager. "How long do you want 'em?"

Jethro scratched his beard. "Uh . . . I guess I better check." And he returned to the truck for another long conversation with C.W. At last, he came back to the manager and said, "A long time. We're building us a house."

What's the last thing you usually hear before a redneck dies?

"Hey y'all . . . Watch this!"

Three redneck construction workers were at a site in Louisiana, sitting on a crossbeam together having lunch.

Billy Joe opened his lunch box and cried, "I don't believe it—a tuna sandwich again! If I get another tunafish sandwich again tomorrow, I swear I'm gonna climb up the scaffolding and jump off!"

Bubba opened his lunch box and exclaimed, "A cheese sandwich again? If I get another cheese sandwich again tomorrow, I'm gonna jump off this building!"

Homer opened his lunch box and said, "Oh, no! Another ham sandwich! If I get another ham sandwich tomorrow, I'm gonna climb up the scaffolding and jump off too!"

The following day, the three sat down to lunch again. Billy Joe opened his lunch box. "I don't believe it—tuna!" he cried. With that, he climbed up the scaffolding and jumped to his death.

Bubba opened his lunch box next. "Damn! Cheese!" He, too, clambered up the scaffolding and leapt to his death.

Homer finally opened his lunch box. "Oh, no! Ham!" And Homer climbed the scaffolding and plummeted to his death.

A few days later, the funeral for the three friends was held. The preacher tried to comfort the windows. Billy Joe's widow seemed utterly inconsolable. "I don't understand, Preacher. If he had only said something—told me he didn't want tuna—I would have given him something different! But he said nothing!"

Bubba's widow wept on the preacher's shoulder. "I don't understand this either," she blubbered. "If Bubba had just told me, I would have made him whatever he wanted."

The preacher made his way over to Homer's widow, who was crying and wailing the loudest of all. "I *really* don't get it!" she exclaimed. "Homer always made his own sandwiches!"

Arkansas Jokes

Did you hear about the new $3 million Arkansas State Lottery?

The winner gets $3 a year for a million years.

Why do folks from Arkansas go to the movie theater in groups of eighteen or more?

The sign said, "Seventeen and under not admitted."

What do you get when you have thirty-two Arkansas lawyers in the same room?

A full set of teeth.

Why did O.J. Simpson want to move to Arkansas?

Everyone has the same DNA.

The Arkansan and his gal were embracing passionately in the front seat of the car. "Want to go in the backseat?" she asked.

"No," he replied.

A few minutes later she asked, "Now do you want to get in the backseat?"

"No," he said again, "I wanna stay here in the front seat with you."

Why do redneck dogs have flat noses?

From chasing parked cars.

A young ventriloquist is touring the clubs and stops to entertain at a bar in a small town. He's going through his usual stupid redneck jokes, when a big burly guy in the audience stands up and says, "I've heard just about enough of your smart-ass hillbilly jokes; we ain't all stupid around here."

Flustered, the ventriloquist begins to apologize, when

the big guy pipes up, "You stay out of this, mister, I'm talking to the smart-ass little fella on your knee!"

A young redneck, going through the fourth grade for the third time, was busy bragging to his friends at school that he knew all the state's capitals by heart.

"Go ahead," he said proudly. "Ask me any one. I know 'em all."

"Okay," one friend said. "What's the capital of Wisconsin?"

"That's easy!" the lad replied. "W."

C.W. was showing off his new apartment in the big city to his friends.

"Say, what's that big brass basin for?" asked Diddles, pointing to a sink leaning against a wall.

"Why, don't you know? That's a talking clock," C.W. replied.

"A talking clock?" Diddles cried. "I don't believe you. How's it work?"

"Watch," said C.W. He picked up a sledgehammer next to the clock and took a crashing swing at the basin.

A voice from the other side of the wall screamed, "Knock it off, you idiot! It's two A.M.!"

Things You Would *Never* Hear a Redneck Say

I'll take Shakespeare for a thousand, Alex.

Duct tape won't fix that.

Come to think of it, I'll have a Heineken.

Has anybody seen the sideburn trimmer?

You can't feed that to the dog.

I thought Graceland was tacky.

No kids in the back of the pickup; it's not safe.

Honey, did you mail that donation to Greenpeace?

We're vegetarians.

Do you think my hair is too big?

Give me the *small* bag of pork rinds.

Deer heads detract from the decor.

I just couldn't find a thing at Wal-Mart today.

Trim the fat off that steak.

The tires on that truck are too big.

I'll have the arugula and radicchio salad with lemon-sherry vinaigrette.

I'd like my fish poached.

My fiancée, Betty Jo, is registered at Tiffany's.

Little Debbie snack cakes have too many saturated fat grams.

Checkmate.

She's too old to be wearing a bikini.

Hey, here's an episode of *Hee Haw* that we haven't seen.

I don't have a favorite college team.

I believe you cooked those green beans too long.

Those shorts ought to be a little longer, Darla.

Elvis who?

C.W. was speaking with his ailing ninety five-year-old mother about the inevitable funeral arrangements for her. "I know you don't wanna talk about this stuff, Ma, but we gotta make some plans fer yer funeral."

His mother was silent, so C.W. continued. "Fer instance, when you die, do you wanna be buried or do you wanna be cremated?"

The old woman thought for a moment, and then replied, "I don't rightly know, C.W. Why don't you just surprise me?"

Religion

A minister died and found himself standing in line waiting to be judged and admitted to heaven.

While waiting, he asked the man in front of him about himself. "I'm a taxi driver from Noo Yawk Cidy," the fellow replied.

Suddenly the angel standing at the gate called out, "Next," and the taxi driver stepped up. The angel handed him a golden staff and a cornucopia of fruits, cheeses, and wine and let him pass. The taxi driver was quite pleased, and he proceeded through the gates.

Next, the minister stepped up to the angel and the angel handed him a wooden staff and some bread and water. The minister was very perplexed, and he asked the angel, "That guy is a taxi driver and gets a golden staff and a cornucopia! I spend my entire life as a minister and get nothing! How can that be?"

The angel replied, "Up here, we judge on results. All of your people sleep through your sermons. In his taxi, they pray."

The priest was preparing a man for his long day's journey into night. Whispering firmly, the priest said, "Denounce the devil! Let him know how little you think of his evil!"

The dying man said nothing.

The priest repeated his order.

Still the dying man said nothing.

The priest asked, "Why do you refuse to denounce the devil and his evil?"

The dying man said, "Until I know where I'm heading, I don't think I ought to aggravate *anybody*."

A man arrives at the gates of heaven. St. Peter asks, "Religion?"

The man says, "Methodist." St. Peter looks down his list, and says, "Go to room twenty-four, but be very quiet as you pass room eight."

Another man arrives at the gates of heaven.

"Religion?"

"Baptist."

"Go to room eighteen, but be very quiet as you pass room eight."

A third man arrives at the gates.

"Religion?"

"Jewish."

"Go to room eleven, but be very quiet as you pass room eight."

The man says, "I can understand there being different rooms for different religions, but why must I be quiet when I pass room eight?"

St. Peter tells him, "Well, the Catholics are in room eight, and they think they're the only ones here."

Rabbi Freiberg sat alone in the sanctuary of his synagogue, clutching a prayer book in his hands and sobbing. "Why, Lord?" he cries out. "Why did this have to happen? How could my son, my *only* son, destroy me like this? My only son—he converted to Christianity!"

And a great voice boomed down from the heavens: *"Yours too?"*

A Christian was thrown into the Coliseum with a lion. Terrified, he fell on his knees and started praying. At the same time the lion dropped down on its knees and started praying, too.

The Christian, overjoyed, exclaimed, "Thank God! Another Christian!"

The lion replied, "I don't know about you, but I'm saying grace."

Two Irishmen were digging a ditch directly across from a brothel. Suddenly, they saw a rabbi walk up to the front door, glance around, and duck inside.

"Ah, will you look at that?" one ditchdigger said. "What's our world comin' to when men of th' cloth are visitin' such places?"

A short time later, a Protestant minister walked up to the door and quietly slipped inside. "Do you believe that?" the other workman exclaimed. "Why, 'tis no wonder th' young people today are so confused, what with the example clergymen set for them."

After an hour went by, the men watched as a Catholic priest quickly entered the brothel. "Ah, what a pity," the first digger said, leaning on his shovel. "One of th' poor lasses must be ill."

Jesus was walking by a village square when he saw a woman tied up in the middle of a crowd. "What is going on?" he asked.

"This woman is a prostitute, and we shall stone her!"

Jesus replied, "Let he who is without sin cast the first stone!"

Everyone slowly walked away, until one middle-aged woman was left. She lifted a heavy brick and threw it, hitting the prostitute on the head and killing her.

Jesus turned to her in exasperation and said, "Sometimes you really piss me off, Mom!"

Three pastors in the south were having lunch in a diner.

One said, "You know, since summer started I've been having trouble with all these bats in my loft and attic at church. I've tried everything—noise, spray, traps, cats—nothing seems to scare them away."

Another said, "Yeah, me too. I've got hundreds living in my belfry and in the attic. I've even had the place fumigated, and they still won't go away."

The third said, "Well, I baptized all mine, and made them members of the church. Haven't seen one back since!"

An elderly priest invited a young priest over for dinner.

During the meal the young priest couldn't help noticing how attractive the housekeeper was. Over the course of the evening he started to wonder if there was more between the elderly priest and the housekeeper than met the eye.

Reading the young priest's thoughts, the elderly priest volunteered, "I know what you must be thinking, but I assure you my relationship with my housekeeper is strictly professional."

About a week later the housekeeper approached the elderly priest and said, "I can't find your beautiful silver gravy ladle ever since that young Father came to dinner. You don't suppose he took it, do you?"

The priest said, "Well, I would very much doubt it, but I'll write him a note just to make sure."

So he sat down and wrote: "Dear Father, I'm not saying you *did* take my silver gravy ladle, and I'm not saying you *did not* take the ladle, but the fact remains it has been missing ever since you came here for dinner."

Several days later he received a reply letter from the

young priest, which read: "Dear Father, I'm not saying you *do* sleep with your housekeeper, and I'm not saying you *do not* sleep with your housekeeper, but if you were sleeping in your own bed you would have found your gravy ladle by now."

A Catholic priest was feeling despondent over being posted to a dry, desert parish. He wrote letters to his bishop constantly, requesting that he be posted somewhere more hospitable. No reply to his letters ever came, and soon the letters stopped.

Sometime later, when the archbishop was making the rounds of the rural churches, he stopped in to see how the unhappy priest was doing. He found a pleasant man, in an air-conditioned church. There were no parishioners, since the closest neighbors were many miles away. The archbishop admitted to some confusion, since the priest did not look like the desperate writer of so many letters. He asked the priest how he liked it out in the desert.

"At first I was unhappy. But thanks to two things I have grown to love it out here in the sparse desert."

"And they are?" the archbishop inquired.

"The first is my Rosary. Without my Rosary I wouldn't make it a day out here."

"And the second?"

At this the priest looked askance. "Well, to be honest, I have developed a taste for martinis in the afternoon. They help to alleviate the heat during the worst part of the day." He looked sheepish at this admission, but the archbishop just smiled.

"Martinis, eh? Well, that's not so bad. In fact, I'd be glad to share one with you right now—if you don't mind, that is."

"Not at all!" the priest exulted. "Let me get one for you right away." Turning to the back of the church, the priest shouted, "Oh, Rosary!"

These Are Actual Announcements from Real Church Bulletins.

Don't let worry kill you—let the church help.

Thursday night: Potluck supper. Prayer and medication to follow. Remember in prayer the many who are sick of our church and community.

For those of you who have children and don't know it, we have a nursery downstairs.

The rosebud on the altar this morning is to announce the birth of David Alan Belzer, the sin of Rev. and Mrs. Julius Belzer.

This afternoon there will be a meeting in the south and north ends of the church. Children will be baptized at both ends.

Tuesday at 4 P.M. there will be an ice-cream social. All ladies giving milk will please come early.

Wednesday the ladies' liturgy will meet. Mrs. Johnson will sing "Put Me in My Little Bed," accompanied by the pastor.

Thursday at 5 P.M. there will be a meeting of the Little

Mothers Club. All ladies wishing to be "Little Mothers" will meet with the pastor in his study.

This being Easter Sunday, we will ask Mrs. Lewis to come forward and lay an egg on the altar.

The service will close with "Little Drops of Water." One of the ladies will start quietly and the rest of the congregation will join in.

Next Sunday a special collection will be taken to defray the cost of the new carpet. All those wishing to do something on the new carpet will come forward and do so.

The ladies of the church have cast off clothing of every kind. They can be seen in the church basement Saturday.

At the evening service tonight, the sermon topic will be "What Is Hell?" Come early and listen to our choir practice.

The preacher will preach his farewell message, after which the choir will sing "Break Forth with Joy."

Today . . . Christian Youth Fellowship House Sexuality Course, 8 P.M. Please park in the rear parking lot for this activity.

During the absence of our pastor, we enjoyed the rare privilege of hearing a good sermon when A. B. Doe supplied our pulpit.

The Rev. Adams spoke briefly, much to the delight of his audience.

The church is glad to have with us today as our guest

minister the Rev. Shirley Green, who has Mrs. Green with him. After the service we request that all remain in the sanctuary for the Hanging of the Greens.

St. Peter got fed up with standing at the Pearly Gates and giving or denying access to heaven, and Jesus offered to take over.

Presently, a man came up to him. "I'm looking for my son," he said.

"And who are you?" asked Jesus.

"I suppose I'm the closest thing he has to a father," said the man.

"What do you do?" asked Jesus curiously.

"I suppose you could say I'm a carpenter," said the man.

"And does your son have holes in his hands and feet?" asked Jesus excitedly.

"He does!" shouted the man.

"Father!" cried Jesus.

"Pinocchio!" shouted Geppetto.

The Pope, Billy Graham, and Oral Roberts were in a three-way plane crash over the Atlantic Ocean. Tragically, they all died and went to the Pearly Gates together.

"Oh, this is terrible," exclaimed St. Peter, "I know you guys think we summoned you here, but this is just one of those coincidences that happen." He fretted. "And since we weren't expecting you all at the same time, your quarters just aren't ready. We can't take you in just yet, and we can't send you back." Then he got an idea. He picked up the phone. "Lucifer, this is Pete. Hey, I got these three guys up here. They're ours, but we weren't expecting them, and we gotta fix the place up for 'em. I was hoping you could put them up for a while. It'll be only a couple of days. I'll owe you one."

Reluctantly, the devil agreed.

But two days later, St. Peter's phone rang. "Pete, this is Lucifer. Hey, you gotta come get these three clowns. This Pope fellow is forgiving everybody, the Graham guy is saving everybody, and that Oral Roberts has raised enough money to buy air-conditioning."

The Pope died and, naturally, went to heaven. He was met by the reception committee, and after a whirlwind tour, he was told that he could enjoy any of the myriad of recreations available.

The Pope decided that he wanted to read all of the ancient original text of the Holy Scriptures, so he spent the next eon or so learning languages. After becoming a linguistic master, he sat down in the library and began to pore over every version of the Bible, working back from most recent "Easy Reading" to the original manuscript.

All of a sudden there was a scream in the library. The angels came running in only to find the Pope huddled in his chair, crying to himself and muttering, "An 'r'! The scribes left out the 'r'!"

A particularly concerned angel took him aside, offering comfort, and asked him what he meant.

After collecting his wits, the Pope sobbed again, "It's the letter 'r.' They left out the 'r.' The word was supposed to be *'celebrate.'* "

A rather dim-witted man saw a priest walking down the street and noticed his unusual collar. He stopped him and said, "Excuse me, but why do you have your shirt on backward?"

The priest laughed. "Because, my son, I am a Father!"

The man was still puzzled. "I'm a father, too," he said, "and I don't wear my shirt backward."

Again the priest laughed. "But I am a Father of thousands," he explained.

"Well, then," the man said, "maybe you should wear your shorts backward instead."

What did the Buddhist say to the hot dog vendor?

Make me one with everything.

A minister had worked himself up into quite a state while delivering a sermon on heaven and hell. "Stand up if you want to go to heaven!" he entreated his congregation.

Everyone in the church rose at once, except a fellow in the front row.

"Are you telling me that you don't want to go to heaven when you die?" the minister asked the man.

"When I die, sure," the man replied. "I thought you were getting up a load to go right now."

An old man goes into a confession booth and tells the priest, "Father, I'm eighty years old, married, have four kids and eleven grandchildren, and last night I had an affair and I made love to two eighteen-year-old girls. Both of them. Twice."

The priest said, "Well, my son, when was the last time you came to confession?"

"Never, Father, I'm Jewish."

"So then, why are you telling me?"

"I'm telling everybody!"

A man who smelled like a distillery flopped onto a subway seat next to a priest. The man's tie was stained, his face was plastered with red lipstick, and a half-empty bottle of gin was sticking out of his torn coat pocket. He opened his newspaper and began reading. After a few minutes the disheveled guy turned to the priest and asked, "Say, Father, what causes arthritis?"

"Mister, it's caused by loose living, being with cheap, wicked women, drinking too much alcohol, and having a contempt for your fellow man."

"Well, I'll be damned," the drunk muttered, returning to his paper.

The priest, thinking about what he had said, nudged the man and apologized. "I'm very sorry. I didn't mean to come on so strong. How long have you had arthritis?"

"I don't have it, Father. I was just reading here that the Pope does."

Three men of the cloth—a Catholic priest, a Baptist minister, and a rabbi—were counting collections taken during services for the week. They were trying to come up with an equitable way to divide the money between God (the two churches and one synagogue) and themselves (the clerics' weekly income).

The priest was the first to speak: "I know what! I'll draw a line down the middle of the sanctuary, toss the money up in the air, and whatever falls on the right side of the line is for God and whatever falls on the left side is for us."

The Baptist minister cried, "No! No! No! I'll draw a circle in the middle of the sanctuary, toss the money up in the air, and whatever falls inside the circle is for God and whatever falls outside the circle is for us."

The rabbi then asked the two other men to accompany him outside. There he offered this suggestion: "What I would do with the money is this: Toss it up in the air, and whatever God catches is His and whatever falls on the ground is ours."

One Sunday morning, the pastor noticed little seven-year-old Johnny was standing staring up at the large plaque that hung in the foyer of the church. The young fellow had been staring at the plaque for some time, so the pastor walked up and stood beside him, and, gazing up at the plaque, he said quietly, "Good morning, son."

"Good morning, pastor," replied the young man without taking his eyes off the plaque. "Sir, what is this?"

"Well, son, these are all the people who have died in the service," replied the pastor.

Soberly, they stood together staring up at the large plaque.

Johnny's voice barely broke the silence when he asked quietly, "Which one sir, the eight-thirty or the ten-thirty?"

Contrary to popular belief, it wasn't the apple on the tree that got us banished from Paradise. It was the pair on the ground.

Sports

A man's wife asked him to go to the store to buy her some cigarettes. So he walked down to the store, only to find it closed.

He went into a nearby bar to get cigarettes from the vending machine. At the bar he noticed a beautiful woman, and he started talking to her. They had a couple of drinks, one thing led to another, and they ended up in her apartment.

After they had their fun, he realized it was 3 A.M. "Oh, no!" he cried. "It's so late, my wife's going to kill me. Have you got any talcum powder?"

She gave him some talcum powder, which he proceeded to rub on his hands. Then he went home.

His furious wife was waiting for him in the doorway. "Where the hell have you been?! I was about to call the police."

"Well, honey, it's like this. I went to the store like you asked, but they were closed. So I went to the bar to use the vending machine. I saw this great-looking woman there, we had a few drinks, and one thing led to another and I ended up in bed with her."

"Oh, yeah? Let me see your hands!" She saw that his hands were covered with powder. "You damned liar! You went bowling again!"

A man died and went to heaven. After reaching the gates to heaven, the man asked St. Peter, "I know I was good during my life, and I really appreciate being brought to heaven, but I'm really really curious. . . . What does hell look like?"

So St. Peter thought about it a moment and finally said, "I'll tell you what, I'll let you see what hell looks like before you are officially entered into heaven. Come with me."

And so St. Peter led the man to an elevator and said, "Take this elevator to the very bottom floor. When the door opens you will see what hell looks like, but whatever you do, do not get out of the elevator."

"Thank you," replied the man, and he climbed into the elevator and hit the button for the lowest floor.

After nearly an hour waiting in the elevator, the doors opened and the man peered out. Before him was a lifeless frozen wasteland. All the man could see were huge mountains of ice through blankets of snow. Remembering what St. Peter said, the man quickly pushed the button for the top floor, the doors closed, and he traveled back up to heaven.

After returning to heaven the man approached St. Peter and said, "I'm ready to enter into heaven now, but before I do I have just one more question."

"Go ahead," replied St. Peter.

The man asked, "I thought hell would be fire and brimstone, but instead all I saw was snow and ice. Is that what it's really like?"

St. Peter thought about this for a second and finally answered, "Snow and ice, huh? I guess the Buffalo Bills finally won the Super Bowl."

Understanding Golf

In primitive society, when native tribes beat the ground with clubs and yelled, it was called witchcraft; today, in civilized society, it is called golf.

The man who takes up golf to get his mind off his work soon takes up work to get his mind off golf.

Golf was once a rich man's sport, but now it has millions of poor players!

Golf is an expensive way of playing marbles.

The secret of good golf is to hit the ball hard, straight, and not too often.

There are three ways to improve your golf game: take lessons, practice constantly—or start cheating.

An amateur golfer is one who addresses the ball twice—once before swinging, and once again, after swinging.

Many a golfer prefers a golf cart to a caddy because it cannot count, criticize, or laugh.

Golf is a game in which the slowest people in the world are those in front of you, and the fastest are those behind.

Golf got its name because all of the other four-letter words were taken.

Great FSU coach Bobby Bowden died and entered the Pearly Gates. God took him on a tour. He showed Bowden a little two-bedroom house with a faded Seminole banner hanging from the front porch. "This will be your house, Coach. Most people don't get their own houses up here," God said.

Bowden looked at the house, then turned around and looked at the mansion sitting on top of the hill. It was huge, with two stories and white marble columns and little patios under every window. University of Florida flags lined both sides of the sidewalk and a huge Gators banner hung between the marble columns.

A bit dejected at the size of the other house, Bowden said, "I didn't know Steve Spurrer died."

"He didn't," God said. "That's my house."

A young man who was an avid golfer found himself with a few hours to spare one afternoon. He figured if he hurried and played very fast, he could get in nine holes before he had to head home.

Just as he was about to tee off, an older gentleman shuffled onto the tee and asked if he could accompany the young man, as he was golfing alone. Unable to say no, he allowed the old gent to join him.

To his surprise the old man played fairly quickly. He didn't hit the ball far, but plodded along consistently and didn't waste much time.

Finally, they reached the ninth fairway, and the young man found himself with a tough shot. There was a large pine tree right in front of his ball—and directly between his ball and the green.

After several minutes of debating how to hit the shot, he heard the old man say, "You know, when I was your age I'd hit the ball right over that tree."

With that challenge placed before him, the youngster swung hard, hit the ball up, right smack into the top of the tree trunk, and it thudded back on the ground not a foot from where it had originally lain.

The old man offered one more comment: "Of course, when I was your age that pine tree was only three feet tall."

A guy stood over his tee shot for what seemed an eternity, looking up, looking down, measuring the distance, figuring the wind direction and speed. It was all driving his partner nuts.

Finally his exasperated partner said, "What the hell is taking so long? Hit the goddamn ball!"

The guy answered, "My wife is up there watching me from the clubhouse. I want to make this a perfect shot."

"Well, hell, man, you don't stand a snowball's chance in hell of hitting her from here!"

Sid and Barney headed out for a quick round of golf. Since they were short on time, they decided to play only nine holes. Sid said to Barney, "Let's say we make the time worth the while, at least for one of us, and spot five dollars on the lowest score for the day."

Barney agreed, and they enjoyed a great game. After the eighth hole, Barney was ahead by one stroke, but he cut his ball into the rough on the ninth. "Help me find my ball; you look over there," he said to Sid.

After five minutes, neither had any luck, and since a lost ball carried a four-point penalty, Barney pulled a ball from his pocket and tossed it to the ground. "I've found my ball!" he announced triumphantly.

Sid looked at him forlornly, "After all the years we've been friends, you'd cheat me on golf for a measly five bucks?!?"

"What do you mean cheat? I found my ball sitting right here!"

"And a liar, too!" Sid said with amazement. "I'll have you know I've been standing on your ball for the last five minutes!"

One day, a man and his wife went golfing, as they frequently did together. They arrived at the twelfth hole, where the husband promptly hit a tremendous slice that ended up behind an old barn.

"I guess I will just have to play it safe and chip onto the fairway," said the man.

"No, wait," replied the wife, who went up to the barn and opened the large doors. "You can hit the ball through the barn."

The man decided to give it a try. But he sliced the ball, which ricocheted off the barn and struck his wife in the head, killing her instantly.

The man was distraught and wallowed in his misery for many weeks, depriving himself of golf the whole time. Eventually he realized that he must face his demons and headed out to the very same golf course to play.

Once again he found himself at the twelfth hole and once again he hit a slice right behind the very same barn.

As he was preparing to hit out safely to the fairway, one of the other players in his foursome remarked, "Why not try to hit it through the barn?"

"Oh, no," replied the man. "I tried that last time."

"What happened?"

"I shot an eight!"

What do Michael Jackson and the Chicago Cubs have in common?

They both wear one glove for no reason.

The Rev. Francis Norton woke up Sunday morning and saw that it was an exceptionally beautiful and sunny early spring day. He decided he simply had to play golf. So he told the associate pastor that he was feeling sick and convinced him to say mass for him that day.

As soon as the associate pastor left the room, Father Norton headed out of town to a golf course about forty miles away. This way he knew he wouldn't accidentally meet anyone he knew from his parish.

Setting up on the first tee, he was alone. After all, it was Sunday morning, and everyone else was in church.

At about this time, St. Peter leaned over to God while looking down from the heavens and exclaimed, "You're not going to let him get away with this, are you?"

God sighed, and said, "No, I guess not."

Just then Father Norton hit the ball, and it shot straight toward the pin, dropping just short of it, then rolling up and falling into the hole. It was a 420-yard hole-in-one!

St. Peter was astonished. He looked at God and asked, "Why did you let him do that?"

God smiled and replied, "Who's he going to tell?"

Bob received a free ticket to the Super Bowl from his company. Unfortunately, when Bob arrived at the stadium he realized the seat was in the last row in the corner of the stadium. He was closer to the Goodyear Blimp than the field!

About halfway through the first quarter, Bob noticed an empty seat ten rows off the field right on the 50 yard line. He decided to take a chance and made his way through the stadium and around the security guards to the empty seat.

As he sat down, he asked the gentleman sitting next to him, "Excuse me, is anyone sitting here?"

The man said, "No."

Very excited to be in such a great seat for the game, Bob said to the man next to him, "This is incredible! Who in their right mind would have a seat like this at the Super Bowl and not use it?!"

The man replied, "Well, actually, the seat belongs to me. I was supposed to come with my wife, but she passed away. This is the first Super Bowl we haven't been to together since we got married in 1967."

"That's really sad," said Bob, "but still, couldn't you find someone to take the seat? A relative or a close friend?"

"No," the man replied, "they're all at the funeral."

The United States

Reliable Indications That You're from New York

You say "the city" and expect everyone to know that this means Manhattan.

You secretly envy cabbies for their driving skill.

You have never been to the Statue of Liberty or the Empire State Building.

You can get into a four-hour argument about how to get from Columbus Circle to Battery Park at 3:30 on the Friday before a long weekend, but can't find Wisconsin on a map.

The subway makes sense.

The subway should never be called anything prissy, like the Metro.

You believe that being able to swear at people in their own language makes you multilingual.

You think $7 to cross a bridge is a fair price.

You've considered stabbing someone just for saying "The Big Apple."

Your door has more than three locks.

You go to a hockey game for the fighting. In the stands. To participate.

Your favorite movie has DeNiro in it.

The most frequently used part of your car is the horn.

You consider eye contact an act of overt aggression.

You call an 8' × 10' plot of patchy grass a yard.

You complain about having to mow it.

You consider Westchester "upstate."

A kindergarten teacher was showing her class an encyclopedia page picturing several national flags. She pointed to the American flag and asked, "What flag is this?"

A little girl called out, "That's the flag of our country."

"Very good," the teacher said. "And what is the name of our country?"

" 'Tis of thee," the girl said confidently.

A Texan in New York City needed to call a nearby community from a pay phone.

"Deposit a dollar and eighty-five cents, please," instructed the operator.

Pulling himself up to full height and using his thickest Texas drawl, he objected, "Ma'am, I'm from Texas, and in Texas we can place a call to hell and back for that price!"

"I understand, sir," retorted the operator, "but in Texas, that's a local call."

The United States, Motto by Motto

Alabama: At Least We're Not Mississippi

Alaska: 11,623 Eskimos Can't be Wrong!

Arizona: But It's a Dry Heat

Arkansas: Litterasy Ain't Everthing

California: As Seen on TV

Colorado: If You Don't Ski, Don't Bother

Connecticut: Like Massachusetts, Only Dirtier and with Less Character

Delaware: We Really Do Like the Chemicals in Our Water

Florida: Ask Us About Our Grandkids

Georgia: We Put the "Fun" in Fundamentalism

Hawaii: Haka Tiki Mou Sha'ami Leeki Toru (Death to Mainland Scum, but Leave Your Money)

Idaho: More Than Just Potatoes . . . Well, Okay, Maybe Not

Illinois: Please Don't Pronounce the "S"

Indiana: 2 Billion Years Tidal Wave Free

Iowa: We Do Amazing Things with Corn

Kansas: First of the Rectangle States

Kentucky: 5 Million People; 15 Last Names

Louisiana: We're Not All Drunk Cajun Wackos, but That's Our Tourism Campaign

Maine: It's Really Cold Here, but We Have Cheap Lobster

Maryland: A Thinking Man's Delaware

Massachusetts: Our Taxes Are Lower Than Sweden's

Michigan: First Line of Defense from the Canadians

Minnesota: Horrible Winters, 10,000 Lakes, and 10,000,000 Mosquitoes

Mississippi: Come Here and Feel Better About Your Own State

Missouri: Your Federal Flood Relief Tax Dollars at Work

Montana: Land of the Big Sky, the Unabomber, Right-Wing Crazies, and Very Little Else

Nebraska: Ask About Our State Motto Contest

Nevada: Let's Play Poker!

New Mexico: Lizards Make Excellent Pets

New York: You Have the Right to Remain Silent, You Have the Right to an Attorney

North Carolina: Tobacco Is a Vegetable

North Dakota: We Really Are One of the 50 States!

Ohio: We Wish We Were in Michigan

Oklahoma: Like the Musical, Only No Singing

Oregon: Spotted Owl . . . It's What's for Dinner

Pennsylvania: Cook with Coal

Rhode Island: We're Not *Really* an Island

South Carolina: Remember the Civil War? We Didn't Actually Surrender

South Dakota: Closer Than North Dakota

Tennessee: The Educashun State

Texas: Si Hablo Ingles (Yes, I Speak English)

Vermont: Yep

Virginia: Who Says Government Stiffs and Slackjaw Yokels Don't Mix?

Washington: Help! We're Overrun by Nerds and Slackers!

Washington, D.C.: Wanna Be Mayor?

West Virginia: One Big Happy Family—Really!

Wisconsin: Come Cut Our Cheese

Wyoming: Wynot?

A pharmacist was giving instructions to a man at his counter. "Take one capsule twice a day with plenty of water," she said. "This medication can make your skin sensitive, so try to avoid exposure to the sun."

He gave her a quizzical look and said, "You're new here in Oregon, aren't you?"

You Know That You Are from California When . . .

The fastest part of your commute is down your driveway.

You were born somewhere else.

You know how to eat an artichoke.

The primary bugs that you worry about are electronic.

Your car has bulletproof windows.

Left is right and right is wrong.

Your monthly house payments exceed your annual income.

If you need a new TV, you can run down to the local riot and pick one up.

You dive under a desk whenever a large truck goes by.

You can't find your other earring because your son is wearing it.

You drive to your neighborhood block party.

Your family tree contains "significant others."

Your cat has its own psychiatrist.

You go to a tanning salon before going to the beach.

Your blind date turns out to be your ex-spouse.

You pack shorts and a T-shirt for skiing in the snow, and a sweater and a wetsuit for the beach.

Rainstorms or thunder are the lead story for the local news.

You'll reluctantly miss yoga class to wait for the hot tub repairman.

You consult your horoscope before planning your day.

A glass has been reserved for you at your favorite winery.

All highways out of the state say: "Go back."

You Might Be from Wisconsin If . . .

You define summer as three months of bad sledding.

Your definition of a small town is one that only has one bar.

Snow tires come standard on all your cars.

At least 50 percent of your relatives work on a dairy farm.

You have ever gotten frostbitten and sunburned in the same week.

You can identify a Michigan accent.

You know what "cow-tipping" is.

You learned to drive a tractor before the training wheels were off your bike.

"Down south" to you means Chicago.

Traveling coast to coast means going from Lake Superior to Milwaukee.

The "Big Three" means Miller, Old Milwaukee, and PBR.

A brat is something you eat.

You have no problem spelling Milwaukee.

You used to think deer season was included as an official school holiday.

The snow on your roof in August weighs more than you do.

Your idea of creative landscaping is a statue of a cow next to your blue spruce.

You go out for fish fry on every Friday.

You go to work in a snowsuit in the morning and return home wearing shorts.

When you tell someone where you are from, they say, "I thought that was part of Canada."

Your idea of the seasons is winter, spring, and the 4th of July.

You know how to polka.

You think that Lutheran and Catholics *are* the major religions.

Formal wear is a flannel shirt, blue jeans, and a baseball cap.

Your 4th of July family picnic was moved indoors due to frost.

You have more fishing poles than teeth.

You decided to have a picnic this summer because it fell on a weekend.

You Know You Live in San Francisco When . . .

You make $100,000 a year, yet still can't find a place to live.

Your commute time is forty-five minutes and you live eight miles away from work.

You stop asking how much things cost, but ask, "How long will it take?"

You know vast differences between Thai, Vietnamese, Chinese, Japanese, Cantonese, and Korean food.

Your home computer contains mostly hardware/software that is not on the consumer market yet.

You go to "the City" on weekends but don't live there because you like your car.

You lost your alarm clock. You'll get to work when you get there.

You own more than ten articles of clothing that have hardware/software companies printed on them.

You scan yard sales for back issues of *Dr. Dobbs.*

Your workplace vending machines dispense "100% natural twig-bars" right next to Jolt cola and instant-espresso mix.

Here Are Some Ripe Old Nuggets of Minnesota Humor

I came, I thawed, I transferred.

Survive Minnesota and the rest of the world is easy.

If you love Minnesota, raise your right ski.

Minnesota—where visitors turn blue with envy.

Save a Minnesotan—eat a mosquito.

One day it's warm, the rest of the year it's cold.

Minnesota—home of the blond hair and blue ears.

Minnesota—come fall in love with a loon.

Land of many cultures—mostly throat.

Where the elite meet sleet.

Minnesota: CLOSED FOR GLACIER REPAIRS

Land of two seasons: winter is coming, winter is here.

Minnesota—glove it or leave it.

Minnesota—have you jump-started your kid today?

There are only three things you can grow in Minnesota: colder, older, and fatter.

Many are cold, but few are frozen.

Why Minnesota? To protect Ontario from Iowa!

Jack Frost must like Minnesota—he spends half his life there.

Land of 10,000 Petersons.

Land of the ski and home of the crazed.

Ten thousand lakes and no sharks!

In Minnesota ducks don't fly, people do!

What Is an American?

We yell for the government to balance the budget, then take the last dime we have to make the down payment on a car.

We whip the enemy in battle, then give them the shirt off our backs.

We yell for speed laws that will stop fast driving, then won't buy a car if it can't go over a hundred miles an hour.

Americans get scared to death if we vote a billion dollars for education, then are unconcerned when we find out we are spending three billion dollars a year for cigarettes.

We'll spend half a day looking for vitamin pills to make us live longer, then drive ninety miles an hour on slick pavement to make up for lost time.

We tie up our dog while letting our sixteen-year-old son run wild.

We will work hard on a farm so we can move into

town where we can make more money so we can move back to the farm.

In the office we talk about baseball, shopping, or fishing; but when we are out at the game, the mall, or on the lake, we talk about business.

We're the country that has more food to eat than any other country in the world and more diets to keep us from eating it.

We run from morning to night trying to keep our earning power up with our yearning power.

We're supposed to be the most civilized Christian nation on Earth, but we still can't deliver payrolls without an armored car.

We have more marriage counselors than any other country in the world and still have by far the most divorces.

We know the lineup of every baseball team in the American and National Leagues, but we don't know half the words of the "Star-Spangled Banner."